MIMI'S SUNRISE SURPRISE

JOAN M. THOMAS
AUTHOR / ILLUSTRATOR

CLASSIC DAY
PUBLISHING

Seattle, Washington
Portland, Oregon
Denver, Colorado
Vancouver, B.C.
Scottsdale, Arizona
Minneapolis, Minnesota

To: Anne
May all your days be filled
With love, support and peace!
Your true friend,
Joan M. Thomas
06-2009

ISBN: 978-0-9821914-0-8
Library of Congress Control Number: 2009901583

Printed in China by Global PSD

Cover Illustration: Joan M. Thomas
Design: Soundview Design Studio

Scripture taken from the King James Version of the Bible

Classic Day Publishing
2925 Fairview Avenue East
Seattle, Washington 98102
877-728-8837
info@classicdaypub.com

Dedication

To my family and in memory of my parents,
Mr. and Mrs. Peter Edward Regal.

And to those who seek God's will, do His work, live by faith,
and follow His command to "love one another."

"For this is the message that ye heard from the beginning,
that we should love one another."

1 John 3:11

"Reading *Mimi's Sunrise Surprise* one finds themselves transported in time to a simpler place – a place where values and family matter most. What starts as a special relationship between a grandmother and granddaughter becomes a story about relationships – friendship, family, and beyond! This lovely childhood tale is relatable on so many levels – for any child who has been teased for being different, for the family who has sent a loved one to war, for those who make church and family cornerstones in their lives – these lessons of love and life are to be enjoyed by all who turn the pages."

Deanna Hollenbach, Director of Communication
Interprovincial Board of Communication
Moravian Church in North America

"*Mimi's Sunrise Surprise* takes Mimi to her Grandparents' farm for an Easter visit. In this fast-moving story, author, Joan M. Thomas deals with the Easter themes of forgiveness and hope in a creative and imaginative way. There is even a 'surprise ending' to delight young readers."

Rev. David A. Schattschneider, Ph.D.
Dean and Vice President Emeritus
Moravian Theological Seminary

"*Mimi's Sunrise Surprise* is an inspiring, joy-filled story of a young Moravian girl who has discovered the treasure of loving God, her family, and her friends. I was challenged and encouraged as I read how she kept a sparkling outlook through serious disappointments and unexpected surprises. The author has the unique gift of describing her characters so that each one captures your heart. You may end up feeling as I did, as though I was part of that dear family. I was sorry to finish the book, but I knew I would meet all my new friends again each time I picked up *Mimi's Sunrise Surprise* and read it to myself, children or grandchildren."

Hope MacDonald, Author

Acknowledgements

With gratefulness I thank:

- My husband, Dick.
- My sons and daughters-in-law, grandchildren, and great-grandchildren.
- Rev. David A. Schattschneider, Ph. D., Dean and Vice President Emeritus, Moravian Theological Seminary.
- Deanna L. Hollenbach, Executive Director of Communication, Interprovincial Board of Communication, Moravian Church in North America.
- Hope MacDonald, Author.
- The Moravian Northwest Fellowship.
- Maxine and Vern Simmons.
- Barbara Dietterich.

Table of Contents

Preface

Mimi's *Sunrise Surprise* was a delight and joy to write and illustrate. Much of this fiction story is taken from my Moravian roots and life experiences.

Joan M. Thomas and her granddaughter in their Moravian outfits.

PART ONE

The Baskets and Bonnets Tea Party

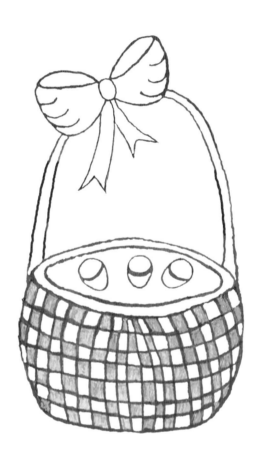

This invitation is sent to you today

Because I want to say
I'd be truly blest
If you would be my guest
At a Baskets and Bonnets Tea Party
This Saturday at Grandma's home
at 3 o'clock.

P.S. Dolls are always welcome!

"Tea parties, dolls, and stories!" Ruth exclaimed, stepping into Grandma's entryway. "I can't think of a better way to spend a rainy Saturday afternoon." She quickly closed Grandma's front door, shutting out the cold April rain and blustery wind and stood her yellow umbrella in the umbrella stand by the door.

"Hello, Ruth," Grandma called from her kitchen over the whirring noise of the eggbeaters. "I'm mixing vanilla frosting for the Scripture cake for our Sunday family dinner. There's a pair of wool slippers in the coat closet. Please put them on if your feet are wet and come join me."

"My shoes are dry, Grandma," Ruth said, sitting her girl doll, Rose, and a bulky brown bag on the entryway table. "I wore boots over my shoes."

From the ceiling Grandma's lighted, crystal Moravian star sent a cascade of glistening rainbow colors dancing merrily on the wall and cast a welcome glow throughout the entryway. Grandma told Ruth it was a Moravian custom to hang the star in the entryway or porch during the Christmas season; however, Grandma was so fond of her star she kept it up all year.

Ruth took off her bright yellow raincoat, wide-brimmed straw hat, and black boots and put them in the closet. Then she glanced in the mirror, smoothed her long, brown hair, and picked up the bag. Holding it with both hands behind her back, she walked from the entryway into Grandma's cheerful kitchen. "Yum! Your house smells scrumptious like cinnamon, chocolate, and fresh baked bread."

"I've got apple dumplings and chicken pot pies baking in the oven for our party," Grandma said. She switched off the electric mixer, looked up, and smiled at Ruth. "And there are hot cross buns, Scripture cake, and whole wheat bread cooling on the counter. Your hot chocolate and my teakettle are heating on the stove." She put the bowl of frosting in the refrigerator, turned toward Ruth, and gave her a hug.

"Dad and Mom said I could stay at your house until it's time for the evening church service."

"Wonderful! That will give you and me more time to enjoy our tea party and story." Grandma smiled broadly. "I woke up early this morning to do the baking and set the dining room table for two with my best china dishes, good silverware, and purple linen napkins. The lights started flickering and the thunder rumbling about an hour ago. I got out the old oil lantern and lit the two beeswax candles on the table in case the power goes off."

Ruth's blue eyes sparkled, and she smiled mischievously. "Grandma, please stop what you're doing and follow me."

"Whatever for?" Bewildered, Grandma placed the dirty eggbeaters in the dishpan in the kitchen sink and wiped her hands on her lavender apron.

Ruth grasped Grandma's hand and led her from the kitchen to the adjacent dining room. "Face the table," she said. "Close your eyes, and don't peek until I count to ten."

Grandma removed her glasses and slipped them into her big apron pocket. "I promise I won't peek," she said, closing her eyes and covering them with her hands.

"One, two, three, four, five." Ruth lifted Grandma's gift from the bag, took a deep breath, and continued counting. "Six, seven, eight, nine, ten." She paused. "Now you can look."

Grandma took her hands down from her face and opened her eyes. "Ooh, my! What a beautiful present." In the middle of her large oak table, between the tall candles, stood a bouquet of bright spring flowers in a red ruby vase and three red Easter eggs in a little basket. "Thank you, honey." Grandma gave Ruth a light kiss on the cheek and put on her glasses.

Ruth beamed. A happy, warm thrill passed from her head to her toes. When Grandma called you "honey," it made you feel special. "I dyed the eggs all by myself," she said proudly.

"The Easter eggs and bouquet are gorgeous," Grandma said. "They'll make a lovely centerpiece for our table."

"Grandma, look!" Ruth put her hands on her hips and twirled merrily around the dining room table like a spinning top. "My dress rustles and swirls when I turn in circles."

"Ruth, be careful," Grandma cautioned. "You look pretty in that long blue dress. But don't get dizzy and trip on the rug."

"I won't." Ruth stopped twirling and laughed. "It's fun to get dressed up for our tea parties." She took a yellow apron from the buffet drawer. "I'm glad you wore that rose dress with your pearls."

"My Grandmother Noble used to say teatime was the most elegant and tranquil time of the day." Grandma grinned. "She always served tea with her finest tea set."

"Grandma, let's have a tea party for my tenth birthday. It's two months away." Ruth pointed to the calendar hanging on the wall. "You'll never guess what I want for my birthday. It's a secret." She paused. "But, I'll tell you." Ruth linked her hand in Grandma's arm and they walked back to the kitchen. Then they leaned their heads together while Ruth whispered in Grandma's ear.

"Oh, my!" Grandma exclaimed. "You want a horse!" Startled, she gasped, took off her glasses, and brushed a strand of her silver-gray hair behind her ear. "Wherever did you get that idea?"

"I know I probably won't get a horse." Ruth sighed. "For my second choice I asked Mom and Dad for either horseback riding lessons or a kitten. Grandma, did you want a horse when you were a girl?"

"With all my heart," Grandma replied. "However when I was your age, World War II wasn't over." She put on her glasses, opened the cupboard by the stove, and lifted her wooden tea caddy from the shelf. "Due to the war, my Dad went to work at the Bethlehem Steel Company. Our family had to move to a small house in Bethlehem, Pennsylvania. The backyard was so tiny, Mom used to say it was the size of a postage stamp. There wasn't any room for a horse, dog, or kitten. But one Easter, when I was just your age, Aunt Lydia gave me horseback riding lessons. That Easter I was in a parade." She chuckled as she chose her special blend of green tea and placed the caddy in the cupboard.

"It must have been awful to move away from your friends," Ruth said, slipping the apron around her waist and tying the strings with a bow, "but wasn't it exciting to learn to ride and be in a parade?"

"It was thrilling," Grandma said, "and an Easter I'll always remember." She took the boiling teakettle off the stove and carefully set it on a trivet on the counter.

"That would be a great story to have after our tea party," Ruth said. "I'll get my doll and prop her up in the dining room rocking chair, so she can hear your story." She disappeared into the hall.

"I have a present for you," Grandma called after her. "It's on the piano bench in the living room."

Ruth bounded back to the kitchen carrying her doll and a gaily-decorated Easter basket crammed with homemade candy, cookies, and colored Easter eggs. "I found the present. Thank you. I can hardly wait to share these treats with our family." Ruth set her doll and the basket in the rocker and washed her hands at the sink.

"Yesterday, while Grandpa dyed Easter eggs," Grandma said as she brewed her tea and poured Ruth's hot chocolate into her white teapot, "I made Moravian mints, chocolate peanut butter Easter eggs, and walnut fudge to put in the Easter baskets. I used my Mother's old family recipes."

"Just thinking about your homemade candy makes my mouth water. Let's have some mints with our story," Ruth said, drying her hands on the kitchen towel. She plopped down on the stool at the kitchen counter, and rested her chin on her hands. "Grandma, how did you celebrate Easter when you were a girl?"

"Well, during Holy Week, the week before Easter," Grandma said, arranging her tea set and Ruth's pot of hot chocolate on her pewter tray, "our family attended the evening services at our Moravian church. On Easter, to celebrate Jesus' resurrection, our family got up before the crack of dawn and went to the Sunrise Service." She carried the tea tray to the dining room table. "The music and singing were magnificent."

"After church, on Easter, my brother and I have an egg hunt in our backyard. Did you and Uncle Matt dye eggs and have egg hunts?" Ruth asked.

"It was a family tradition," Grandma replied, standing a loaf of whole-wheat bread on the breadboard, "to dye our Easter eggs on Maundy Thursday." She continued as she sliced the bread. "We had an egg hunt after our Easter church service."

"Egg hunts are fun," Ruth said. She got up from the stool and took a jar of Grandma's homemade apple butter from the refrigerator. "But, what I like best is an Easter parade with a loud band."

"During the war lots of items were scarce. If our town held a parade, all the neighbors and our family would either walk or ride the bus downtown to watch it," Grandma said, stacking the pieces of bread on a tray. "All the ladies wore fancy Easter bonnets to the parade."

"Did you wear a hat?" Ruth put the bread tray and jar of spicy apple butter on the table.

"Oh, my, yes! Hats were in style," Grandma replied. "On Palm Sunday Mom would take our hand-me-down hats out of our old trunk. I'd watch in amazement as she fashioned those shabby hats into stylish Easter bonnets with silk flowers, ribbons, and veils. One year, when our family was visiting Grandpa Noble's farm in Lititz, I decided to decorate my own hat."

"What kinds of decorations did you use?" Ruth asked.

"I spent hours trimming my straw brimmed bonnet with flowers I picked from Grandmother Noble's garden. Later, when I went into the barn proudly wearing my hat to help Grandpa feed the horses, his big Shire horse whinnied, snatched my hat off my head, and gobbled it down for his dinner." She chuckled. "From that day on, I let Mom decorate the hats."

Just then the timer buzzed in the kitchen. "Oh! I forgot the apple dumplings and chicken pot pies were in the oven." Grandma hurried to remove the dumplings and pies from the oven and put them on a large platter.

"Look!" Ruth pointed to the pot pies and laughed. "Steam is shooting out of the holes in the top crust of the pies. They look like erupting volcanoes." Then she glanced down at her wristwatch. "Grandma, our tea party starts in exactly five minutes. We need to get our hats."

Ruth and Grandma quickly took off their aprons, hung them in the kitchen closet, and dashed to the entryway. After putting on their hats, they scurried to the dining room, sat down at the table, and said the Moravian table blessing.

No sooner were they through praying when the grandfather clock in the hall chimed three o'clock.

"Since all the food is on the table," Grandma said, pouring Ruth's hot chocolate, "we can relax and enjoy our tea party."

Ruth took a small bite of the warm chicken pot pie. "Grandma, this pie is delicious! The crust melts in my mouth like butter."

"Good," Grandma said. She tasted the pie and grinned. "The crust is perfect!"

Later, after Ruth and Grandma were through with their meal, Grandma stated, "Now, it's time for some mints, another cup of tea, and our story."

"I'm ready!" Ruth moved her chair closer to Grandma's chair.

Suddenly, outside the storm grew violent. The rain turned to pounding hail. The afternoon sky became coal black. Howling wind shook the flowering dogwood tree by the dining room window.

"Grandma," Ruth cried. "The lights are flickering."

Then a brilliant bolt of lightning lit up the bleak sky immediately followed by a booming crash of thunder.

Darkness engulfed Grandma's home except for her cozy dining room, where the old lantern and beeswax candles continued to shed their light. The sweet smell of the beeswax seemed to fill the room as black shadows danced on the cream-colored walls.

"Having our story by candlelight will be exciting!" Ruth exclaimed.

Grandma took off her glasses and laid them on the table. "Ruth, there's an antique white milk glass bowl and a tarnished gold trophy on the top shelf of my china cabinet. Would you please take them out of the cabinet and set them on the table?"

Ruth stood, walked to the cabinet, and stretched on her tiptoes to reach the top shelf. "Grandma, this bowl's shaped like an Easter basket, and there are two small wooden Easter eggs in the trophy." She carefully lifted the small fragile bowl and trophy off the shelf and put them on the table.

"The eggs are hollow and designed to hold secret keepsakes," Grandma explained. "Please read the words and dates carved on them."

Ruth reached into the trophy, lifted out the eggs, and held them close to the lantern. She wrinkled her brow and squinted in the dim yellow light as she tried to read the words worn smooth with time. "Grandma, I can see an empty cross and the date *Easter 1864* carved on the front of one of the wooden eggs. Inscribed on the other egg are the words: *Easter 1944, Mimi's Sunrise Surprise.*"

"That's right, Ruth. Now, come back with me in time," Grandma said, over the rumbling thunder and sleet beating on the windows, "to that memorable Easter in 1944 when I learned to ride horseback and received a special sunrise surprise."

PART TWO

Grandma's Story:
"Mimi's Sunrise Surprise"

CHAPTER ONE

Aunt Lydia's Letter

"Mom, I'm home from school! Our Easter vacation starts tomorrow. I don't have to go back to school for two weeks." I closed the kitchen back door and pointed to the calendar dated March 1944 hanging on the wall. Then I plopped my book bag and metal lunch box on the kitchen table and took off my red jacket. Embroidered on my jacket's corduroy collar were my initials: M. N. for Mimi Noble. "Is Matt home?" I asked as I hung my jacket in the hall closet.

Mom stopped peddling the treadle sewing machine in the corner of the kitchen, looked up from her mending, and smiled. "No, Mimi. Dad drove him to his art class," she said. "They won't be home until supper time." Bits of thread and scraps of cloth were scattered on the floor, and a large basket of mended clothes stood next to the sewing machine. Matt was my big brother. He was three years older and four inches taller than me. Everybody said he looks like Dad with his blue eyes and sandy-colored hair. My eyes and hair were dark brown like Mom's. Matt wanted to be a sculptor when he grew up.

"My teacher corrected our history reports," I said. "She wrote on my paper that I showed improvement in spelling and demonstrated excellent use of my imagination." Spelling and arithmetic weren't my favorite subjects. I loved reading and history. I hugged Mom and handed her my report.

"I'm proud of you, honey," Mom said. "There's a letter for you on the kitchen table from Aunt Lydia. When Mr. Sampson delivered our mail, he mentioned that he was going to ask you to watch Mom-Cat while he's on his Easter vacation."

"I wonder why Aunt Lydia wrote to me," I said, looking at the white envelope on the table.

"You can read her letter after you change your clothes. On your way upstairs, please put Dad's mail on the living room table by his leather chair." Mom smiled, gave me the mail, and resumed sewing. "Mimi, don't forget your book bag," she called after me as I headed for the living room.

When we moved into this house in Bethlehem because of Dad's job and the war, I chose the smallest bedroom since it had a window seat where I could snuggle up with my books, read, write stories, and dream. Grandpa Noble built my maple bookcases, table, and chairs.

Grandmother helped me make a round needlepoint sampler to hang on my wall. The phrase I embroidered was my favorite, "Love One Another."

Once in my room, I scooped up my teddy bear and Moravian doll, Patience, from off my bed and hugged them. Patience and my teddy bear were my good friends. I propped them up on the pillows at the head of my bed, changed into my play clothes, and went downstairs.

"Mom, I have to go outside to feed Clef and Codetta," I said, getting the birdseed from the pantry. "I fed Plodder this morning." Plodder was my pet turtle. Clef and Codetta were two little sparrows. They lived in a birdhouse our family built in the backyard.

"Good work, Mimi," Mom said after I fed the sparrows. She handed me Aunt Lydia's letter. Mom had four sisters and no brothers. Aunt Lydia, Mom's youngest sister, was married to Uncle Jim, my Dad's younger brother. They lived with Grandpa and Grandmother Noble in Lititz, Pennsylvania. Uncle Jim helped Grandpa with the farm. When the war broke out, he enlisted in the Army. Aunt Lydia continued living at the farm. Uncle Jim and Aunt Lydia owned three horses and a yard goods shop. Mom's oldest sister, Aunt Hannah, was married to Uncle Luke. They lived in Lititz, too. Our other relatives lived in Nazareth.

"Thanks, Mom." I opened the envelope. "I'll read the letter to you:

Dear Mimi,

Would you like to spend your Easter vacation at the farm and help me at the shop? It's time to order the summer fabrics, and I'd appreciate your assistance. Grandmother is occupied with church activities and spring-cleaning. Aunt Hannah has a full schedule as the church organist and teaching needlepoint and music.

In our spare time, I'll give you horseback riding lessons. The town is planning an Easter parade the Saturday before Easter. We could make an Easter banner, and you could carry it leading the parade riding Graceful Lady. I'd ride behind you, mounted on Freedom. Our horses never fail to win a gold trophy. If you decide to come, Grandpa and Grandmother Noble can drive to Bethlehem this Sunday and pick you up at two o'clock. We have the upstairs guest Angel Room ready for you.

Love and hugs, Aunt Lydia

P.S. Please bring your Moravian outfit. Aunt Hannah and Grandmother want to use it as a pattern to sew an outfit for Charity Timothy, one of Aunt Hannah's music students."

I folded the letter and put it in the envelope. "Learning to ride is one of my dreams." I sighed. "The last time we were at Lititz was for Aunt Lydia and Uncle Jim's wedding. That was over seven months ago. Mom, may I please go to the farm?" I coaxed, putting the envelope in my pocket.

Mom stood and closed the lid of the sewing machine. "I think it would be wonderful for you to go to the farm," she said, setting the basket of clothes on her chair. "Remember, if you go you won't be able to help make our Easter gift baskets or be in the children's program at church."

"That's all right," I said, although I loved being in the performances and making our gift baskets.

It was a family tradition to dye and decorate our Easter eggs with colorful symbols of the cross, fish, or angel on Maundy Thursday. While the eggs were drying, Matt and I made little Easter baskets from colored construction paper. Then we tucked an egg, a cross-shaped molasses cookie, and an Easter card our family designed into every basket. On each card we drew an empty cross and printed, "For He is risen!" On Easter morning, we gave the baskets to our relatives and friends. "I would miss that, but I really want to go to the farm."

"You can read Aunt Lydia's letter to Dad this evening. He can call Grandpa with our decision tomorrow morning." Mom glanced at the mantle clock. "It's almost supper time. Dad and Matt will be home soon. We need to bake the cornbread and cook the stuffed cabbage rolls."

"I'll help you, Mom." I pushed the sewing machine into the kitchen closet and took the canisters of flour and corn meal from the cupboard.

"Thank you, Mimi. It won't take long to mix the beef and other ingredients for the rolls." She dropped the cabbage leaves into a pot of water boiling on the stove.

At six o'clock Dad and Matt arrived home. While they got ready for supper, Mom and I took the bread and rolls out of the oven and put them on the kitchen table. Then we all sat down at the table for our meal.

After supper, Matt and Dad carried their dessert of apple crumb pie into the living room. I helped Mom wash and dry the dishes and sweep the kitchen floor. *I wonder what Dad will say when I ask him if I can go to the farm for two weeks*, I thought as Mom and I went into the living room. Dad was relaxing in his leather armchair listening to the radio and sketching in his artist's portfolio. Matt was lounging on the floor molding a little clay angel. Mom sat down on the sofa and began crocheting.

Holding Aunt Lydia's letter in my hand, I marched over to Dad and stood in front of him. "Dad," I said, "excuse me for interrupting you. Aunt Lydia sent me a letter. May I read it to you?" I paused. "Then I need to ask you an important question."

Dad nodded, put his pencil and portfolio on the table, and switched off the radio. He listened while I read the letter.

"Dad, may I please go to Grandpa's farm?" I asked when I finished reading. I gave him the letter, clenched my hands behind my back, and held my breath. I could feel and hear my heart thumping in my chest.

Dad rose from his chair, looked over my head to meet Mom's eyes, and then down at me.

It seemed like an eternity until Dad said, "Mimi, your request is granted." He laughed. "How can I refuse those dark, pleading eyes?"

"Thank you!" I shouted. I clapped my hands and jumped up and down.

"You can spend Easter vacation at the farm," Dad said, sitting back down in his armchair, "if your chores are done, you're all packed by Saturday evening, and you practice your tap dancing while you're there."

"I'll be ready by noon tomorrow," I said. "I promise I'll practice." I loved to dance and was learning a new dance for my dancing school's May Day performance.

"If Grandpa drives you to the farm this Sunday," Dad said, handing me Aunt Lydia's letter, "Mom, Matt, and I will drive to Lititz on the morning of The Great Sabbath, the Saturday before Easter, and stay overnight at the farm. On Easter, after the Sunrise Service, we'll bring you home."

"Hurray!" I exclaimed. Now all I had to do was ask Matt to take care of the sparrows and my turtle for the next two weeks and return my library books. But I didn't have to ask

Matt. He volunteered. "Thank you, Matt, Mom, and Dad," I said. "I'm going to my room to pack." I blew them a kiss and headed for the stairs.

"Mimi, I'll be up in a few minutes with Dad's leather suitcase," Mom called to me.

After I went to my room, I put on my red nightgown and robe. I sat down at my desk and wrote in my diary. *It's Friday. I'm leaving Sunday to spend two weeks at Grandpa and Grandmother Noble's farm. I like to pretend their big stone and wood farmhouse is a castle, the nearby creek a moat, and the stone lions guarding the entranceway are real but friendly. One of my dreams is coming true. Aunt Lydia's going to teach me to ride!*

At the bottom of the page, I drew a picture of me, riding Graceful Lady, decked out in a riding coat and jodhpurs. *I'd love to have a riding outfit,* I thought. I sighed, closed my diary, and put Aunt Lydia's letter into my jewelry chest sitting on my desk. Since the war, any extra money in our family went toward the War Effort and not for luxuries. "Don't worry," I said, hugging my teddy bear and Patience. "You're both going to the farm with me."

When Mom brought Dad's suitcase upstairs, we made a list of the things I needed to take to the farm.

"It's an hour past your bedtime," Mom said as the grandfather clock downstairs chimed ten o'clock. "I'll get your Moravian outfit out of our old trunk tonight. You can pack it with

the rest of your clothes in the morning. Now, hurry and get into bed. After prayers, I'll tell you a story."

"Mom, I'm happy I can go to the farm." I climbed into bed and slid under the covers. "But, I wish the war was over. I want Uncle Jim and our dog, Valiant, to come home." I wrapped my arms around Mom's neck, pulled her close, and whispered, "I miss Valiant and worry about him. Even Grandpa said Valiant was the smartest German Shepherd he had ever seen!" My lips trembled. Hot tears floated in my eyes.

Mom sat down on my bed and gently brushed my tangled hair. "Honey," she said, "Dad and I are proud of you and Matt for loaning Valiant to the K-9 Corps to be a military dog."

"I don't want Valiant to get hurt." I wiped my eyes with my handkerchief.

"We know it was hard for you and Matt to make that decision," Mom said. "Families all around our country are making sacrifices and facing hardships." She held me close and kissed my forehead. "Now, it's time for prayers. We'll thank God for our blessings and ask for wisdom."

"And that people will love one another," I said, pointing to my needlepoint sampler on the wall. "Then the war will end and all the soldiers and military dogs can come home."

After prayers, Mom read the passages that described love from my Bible. Then she told me a story about the founding of Bethlehem, Nazareth, and Lititz, Pennsylvania, by the heroic Moravians, and how the early Moravian missionaries traveled by foot or mounted on horses or donkeys, carrying Bibles and provisions, into the dangerous Pennsylvania territory to take the Gospel to the Indians and settlers.

"Remember, Mimi, you don't have to travel to far away places to do God's work and share His word and love. You can start right where you are to be a good friend and neighbor. Good night, honey." She plumped up my pillow, hugged me, and went downstairs. Drowsy and content, I turned off my bedside lamp and burrowed under the blankets with my doll and teddy bear, but I lay awake until our grandfather clock struck midnight, imagining I was wearing a scarlet riding jacket, tan jodhpurs, and black boots while riding Graceful Lady. In my dreams, I was standing in the winner's circle with a gold trophy held high in my hand.

CHAPTER TWO

Off To The Farm

Despite staying up late the night before, I was the first to awaken on Saturday morning. The house was quiet and still. For a minute as I lay in bed I thought I had dreamed about going to Grandpa's farm for my Easter vacation. Then I remembered Aunt Lydia's letter. Overjoyed, I rolled out of bed and took the envelope from my jewelry chest. Cradling Patience and my teddy bear in my arms, I read them the letter. Just then, I heard Dad shoveling coal to put in the furnace, Mom going downstairs to make breakfast, and Matt stirring in his bedroom.

After we ate breakfast and Dad read the scriptures and prayer from the *Moravian Daily Texts Book*, Matt and I went outside and loaded the newspapers and scrap metal we collected from the neighbors into the trunk of our car. Then Dad and Matt took the metal and papers to our town's Collection Center for the War Effort. Mom and I stayed home and did the Saturday baking. Then I finished packing.

That afternoon, when Mr. Sampson delivered our mail, I ran outside to meet him. Mom-Cat was riding on his shoulder, proud and stately. I told Mr. Sampson I was going to Grandpa Noble's farm in Lititz for my Easter vacation. Mr. Sampson surprised me by saying he grew up in Lititz, and he and Grandpa were good friends. Mr. Sampson said Mom-Cat could go to the farm with me. He'd call Grandpa and tell him I was bringing Mom-Cat.

"Hurray! Thank you, Mr. Sampson," I shouted. "I'll take good care of Mom-Cat, and we have a basket she can use for a bed."

Mr. Sampson stooped, and Mom-Cat jumped from his shoulder to the ground. Mom-Cat looked up at me and meowed her approval. Before continuing on his mail route, Mr. Sampson took our letters from his leather mail pouch and gave them to me.

Later that evening, while Matt and I were playing records on the Victrola in the living room, the city held a blackout drill. During the blackout drill, our family rehearsed what we would do if we had a real air raid. Mom and Dad pulled our dark window shades down and closed the drapes. Matt and I turned off all the lights. When the drill was over, I carried Mom-Cat upstairs to my room and put her basket on the floor by my bed. Mom-Cat meowed, climbed into her cozy basket, and purred contentedly. Then I did my Sunday school lesson and wrote in my diary: *Saturday: My clothes, Bible, journal, Moravian outfit, and tap shoes are packed. Tomorrow I'm off to the farm!*

Exactly at two o'clock on Sunday afternoon, Grandpa and Grandmother Noble arrived. "Grandpa looks distinguished," Mom said proudly as we stood at the kitchen window and watched them get out of their old, black car, "and Grandmother elegant." Grandpa had on a tweed jacket. Grandmother's gray hair was pulled back in a bun, and she was wearing a hat and white gloves.

While I carried Mom-Cat in her basket and Patience out to Grandpa's car, Dad and Grandpa lingered in the kitchen over their coffee and sticky cinnamon buns and discussed what kinds of vegetables to plant in our Victory Garden in the backyard. Mom and Grandmother took their tea in the living room and chatted about church activities. When I came back into the house, Grandmother was standing in the kitchen holding a basket filled with jars of Mom's homemade apple butter and strawberry jam.

Grandpa was peering through his spectacles checking the time on his gold pocket watch. "Mimi, we need to leave in fifteen minutes," he said. "Grandmother and I have to get back to the farm for evening chores."

"I'm ready, Grandpa." I put on my coat, broad-brimmed hat, and grabbed my teddy bear. We all went outside. Matt loaded my luggage in the car, and Grandpa got in the driver's

seat. Grandmother sat next to him. I hugged Mom and Dad, crawled in the back of the car with my teddy bear, and sat down on the seat between Mom-Cat and Patience. Perched in her basket on her royal purple pillow, Mom-Cat looked like a queen. Grandpa started the car. It sputtered and coughed, then suddenly the engine roared! With a backward jolt and a forward lurch, we were on our way. The two small American flags attached to the front fenders of Grandpa's car made a crackling noise as the wind whipped them back and forth. I rolled down the side window, held onto my hat, and poked my head out the window. "Good-bye," I yelled. "I love you." I waved to Mom, Dad, and Matt until Grandpa's car rounded the corner of our street and they were lost from my sight.

CHAPTER THREE

Finding New Friends

The next morning I awoke to the clanging sound of the farm bell, the crowing of the barnyard rooster, and the gentle pitter-patter of rain dripping on the roof. I shoved the warm down coverlet aside and sprang out of the old-fashioned canopy bed. The bouncing mattress woke Mom-Cat, who was sleeping at the foot of the bed. Startled, she gave a loud "meow."

"I'm sorry, Mom-Cat," I said, petting her. I switched on the overhead light and glanced at the hand carved wooden angel clock on the maple dresser. "It's Monday morning and six o'clock. We're at Grandpa's farm. It's time to wake up." I smoothed the rumpled coverlet, hugged Patience and my teddy bear, and set them in the Windsor chair next to the rolltop desk by the window.

Mom-Cat yawned, stretched, and groomed herself with her white paws while I took my blue denim bib overalls and red flannel shirt from my suitcase and got dressed.

Last night, after Grandpa, Grandmother, and I arrived at the farm, we ate supper and did the chores. Later, Aunt Hannah and Uncle Luke stopped by to visit. Uncle Luke was a doctor. Aunt Hannah, the church organist, also taught music and needlepoint. They lived in town and had remodeled the parlor and sitting room of their house into a doctor's office and music studio. Grandpa told me, with a wide grin, that when Uncle Luke's patients had an appointment at his office they also received a large dose of Aunt Hannah's Moravian music. After Uncle Luke and Aunt Hannah went home, I carried my luggage, Mom-Cat, Patience, and my teddy bear upstairs to the guest Angel Room and got ready for bed. Later, Grandmother came upstairs and tucked me into bed. I didn't get to see Aunt Lydia. She was working late at her yard goods shop.

I wonder when my riding lessons will begin, I thought, pulling on my socks and shoes. I quickly brushed and braided my long hair in two pigtails, tied them with red ribbons, and raced to the window. I rolled up the blackout shade, opened the window, and leaned over the sill. The rain had turned to a fine drizzle. Through the mist, I could see Grandpa winding the farm bell's rope around its post. The post from which the bell was hanging and flagpole stood at the end of the back yard. A sea of bluebells surrounded the base of the bell post and flagpole. Beyond the yard was Grandpa's big stone barn and livery stable. Next to it was the outdoor fenced riding arena. Hidden by the apple orchard, in the distance, were the chicken coop and pigpen.

Crystal, Grandpa's English Shepherd, was herding four cows, three sheep, two goats, and a little lamb with a tinkling bell dangling from her collar to the pasture, while Mr. Jason carried milk cans from the cellar to the barn. Mr. and Mrs. Jason were longtime friends and helped Grandmother and Grandpa with the farm work. Their only son was a pilot in the Army Air Forces. I shivered from the cold and quickly closed the window. I tossed my red wool cardigan over my shoulders and ran downstairs. Mom-Cat followed. She promenaded down the steps like a queen visiting her royal subjects.

The tantalizing smells of sausage, eggs, waffles, and Moravian sugar cake led me to Grandmother's large kitchen. Because of the war, lots of items were scarce, but at Grandpa's farm, which yielded all kinds of produce and dairy products, there was always enough food and some to spare for any needy neighbors.

I stopped at the doorway to bask in the warmth coming from Grandmother's black, cast-iron coal stove. Years ago Grandpa had painted the borders of the kitchen doors and cupboards with apple green ivy, pink cabbage roses, and bright tulips.

Grandmother and Mrs. Jason had on gingham aprons, and their faces were rosy pink from the stove's heat. In the corner of the kitchen, Mrs. Jason kneaded bread on the dough tray while Grandmother mixed batter for the waffle iron. Aunt Lydia, sitting at Grandmother's large oval kitchen table, had on tan riding breeches, boots, and a green sweater set. Her short black hair fell onto her cheeks as she bent over a stack of fabric order forms and an open notebook.

Grandpa and Mr. Jason were hanging their yellow raincoats and hats on the clothes rack by the kitchen back door. I held my breath and watched Crystal, who had followed Grandpa into the kitchen carrying a dog biscuit in her mouth, go over to Mom-Cat and drop the biscuit on the floor in front of her. Pretzel, Grandmother's big brown cat, meowed and walked over to greet Mom-Cat. Then these three shared a dish of cream by the icebox. I heaved a sigh of relief, knowing they would be friends.

Grandpa walked over to me, swept me off my feet, and gave me a big bear hug. When he put me down, Mr. and Mrs. Jason shook my hand and welcomed me to the farm. They called me Miss Mimi. No one had ever spoken to me in such a formal way.

"Breakfast will be ready in two minutes," Grandmother said. She smiled at me, poured a cup of the blueberry waffle batter into the steaming waffle iron, and closed the lid.

"Morning, Mimi," Aunt Lydia said cheerfully. "When I got home late last night I peeked in the Angel Room to say hello. You and Mom-Cat were sound asleep." She laughed and her blue eyes twinkled. "We'll leave for my shop after breakfast." She stood and whisked the stack of forms and notebook into her briefcase and put it on the floor by her chair. I adored Aunt Lydia. She was pretty, petite, fun, and loved horses.

Mrs. Jason poured Grandpa's and Mr. Jason's hot black coffee into the biggest white mugs I had ever seen, and Aunt Lydia and I carried the food to the table. Then we all sat down, bowed our heads, and said the Moravian table blessing. After our hearty breakfast, Grandpa read the Bible verses and prayer from the *Moravian Daily Texts Book*. When he was through reading, he closed the book with his large, calloused, work-worn hands and turned toward me. "Mimi, would you like to make any comments?" he inquired.

"Yes, Grandpa," I said. "I wish people would love one another. Then there'd be peace. The war would be over and my dog, Valiant, and all those serving in the military could come home."

Grandpa rose from his chair, planted a kiss on my forehead, and ruffled my bangs. "Honey, that's one of the smartest statements I've heard in a long time." He chuckled. Then Grandpa and Mr. Jason put on their rain jackets and took their mugs of hot coffee and sugar cake outside.

"Mimi, to save gasoline," Aunt Lydia said, "I've been riding my bicycle to town. While you're staying at the farm, you can ride my bike and I'll ride Uncle Jim's. We'll take our dresses and aprons and change at the shop. I'll get the bikes out of the garage while you're getting ready." She rose from her chair and picked up her briefcase. "Monday is always my busiest day. Tomorrow after we come home from the shop, we'll start your horseback riding lessons and design the banner for the town's parade."

Thrilled, I carried my dirty dishes to the sink and bounded up the stairs to the Angel Room. *Riding lessons at last*, I thought. I took my purple dress and yellow apron from my suitcase, rolled, and slid them into my backpack. Then I wrapped Patience in her doll blanket and went down to the kitchen.

"Since you'll be at the shop all day," Grandmother said, handing me a black metal lunchbox, "I packed a lunch for you and Aunt Lydia. This box is filled with all kinds of tasty surprises."

"Thank you, Grandmother." I slipped on my jacket and hat, hugged her, and slung my backpack over my shoulders. I scooped up Mom-Cat snoozing in Grandmother's rocker. Carrying Mom-Cat, Patience, and the lunch box, I went out to the back porch to wait for Aunt Lydia. The drizzling rain had stopped, and the sun was beginning to shine through white cotton clouds. I sat down on the wooden glider and started swinging.

"Before we leave," Aunt Lydia called to me as she emerged from the garage wheeling the bicycles, "would you like to come to the barn and feed the horses some treats?" She parked the bikes in the graveled driveway by the side of the house and headed for the barn.

"Oh, yes!" I leaped from the glider. Holding Patience, Mom-Cat, and the lunchbox, I flew down the porch stairs. "Aunt Lydia, wait for me," I shouted.

As soon as Aunt Lydia and I stepped inside the barn, she pulled a bag of sliced apples and carrots from her coat pocket. The stone barn was huge and smelled sweet like our beeswax candles. Aunt Lydia gave me the bag of apples and carrots, and I fed some of them to her beautiful Tennessee Walking Horse, Graceful Lady. Then I fed the remaining treats to Liberty, Uncle Jim's chestnut thoroughbred, and Freedom, his high-spirited Arabian. Grandpa's two large, powerful Clydesdales and Shire horse were munching oats from their feed buckets. I didn't interrupt their breakfast. I noticed each horse had its name printed on a plaque hanging above the door of its stall. The small end stall was empty, and the plaque was unmarked.

"It's time to go," Aunt Lydia said. She checked the time on the gold watch pendant she wore around her neck and smiled. "I open the shop at nine o'clock every day except Sunday. The shop is closed on Sunday."

We scurried from the barn to the driveway and climbed onto our bikes. I set Mom-Cat in the wire basket attached to the front handlebars and tucked Patience in my backpack. Aunt Lydia put the lunchbox in her bike basket. When I started pedaling, Mom-Cat sneezed, wrinkled her nose, and shook her head back and forth as the wind tickled her whiskers and rippled her fur.

"Aunt Lydia," I said, riding beside her on the winding country road, flanked by towering maple trees and rolling farmland, "why was the last stall in the barn empty?"

"Mr. Jason helps Grandpa with the farm work. He's also a blacksmith. If Mr. Jason needs to have a horse stay overnight, the horse can stay in that stall."

Suddenly, we rounded a sharp curve. In the distance I spotted a man standing in the middle of the road wiping his forehead with a large white handkerchief. A light blue car was parked on the right side of the road.

On the opposite side, in the muddy ditch, lay a donkey tied to a weeping willow tree.

"Look! Aunt Lydia," I shouted. "That man needs help."

"It's Mr. Timothy. He's a pharmacist and works in town at the hospital. Charity, his daughter, is about a year and a half younger than you. His son, Mark, is fifteen. They moved to Lititz four months ago and are members of our church." Aunt Lydia slammed on her brakes. The tires skidded on the wet road as she came to a rapid stop.

"That donkey has the biggest ears I've ever seen." I parked my bike next to Aunt Lydia's and followed her.

"Good morning," Aunt Lydia called to Mr. Timothy. She walked briskly toward him. "This is my niece, Mimi. We're on our way to town to open my shop."

"Hello, Lydia." Mr. Timothy mopped his brow with his handkerchief.

"How do you do, Mr. Timothy?" I said.

"Glad to meet you, Mimi." He tipped his hat, shook my hand, and smiled.

"How can we help you?" Aunt Lydia asked.

"Well, I was driving Charity to town," Mr. Timothy said, "for her doctor's appointment when we noticed Mr. Moses' donkey, Lilly, ambling down the road with her halter on and dragging her rope. I stopped my car and tied her to the tree so she wouldn't wander any farther and get lost." He continued, "Mr. Moses fractured his hip and went to the hospital yesterday morning. Mrs. Moses is recuperating from a bout of pneumonia and visiting their daughter in Nazareth. Evidently no one has been taking care of Lilly. She must have been looking for food and water. I don't want to abandon Lilly; however, I have to get Charity to her doctor's appointment and go to work."

All of a sudden, Mom-Cat soared out of the bike basket. She ran to Lilly, rubbed her pink nose against the donkey's forelock and muzzle, and meowed. Lilly lifted her head, wiggled her big ears, and brayed softly. Then Mom-Cat, who detests being dirty, sat down in the mud beside Lilly, and gazed up at me with questioning eyes.

"Don't be afraid, Lilly." I crouched down, petted her head, and looked into her large, brown, sorrowful eyes. Lilly sighed and rested her head on my arm.

"Be careful!" Mr. Timothy yelled. "She might bite."

"Aunt Lydia, we can't leave Lilly here alone. Grandpa has an empty stall in the barn. Can we please take Lilly to the farm?" I pleaded.

Aunt Lydia's eyes met mine and she smiled. Then she turned toward Mr. Timothy. "Do you have time to drive back to our farm, and ask Grandpa Noble to hook the horse trailer to his truck and get Lilly?"

"I'd be glad to, Lydia," Mr. Timothy said in a relieved tone. He walked toward his car. "Charity and I will feel better knowing the donkey's in good hands."

"Thank you, Aunt Lydia." I scrambled to my feet and hugged her.

"Tell him," Aunt Lydia said, "Mimi found a wilting Lilly on the road to Lititz." She laughed heartily. "And this Lilly needs water, food, and tender, loving care."

As Mr. Timothy turned his car around, a girl with long, blonde curly hair peeked from the car's rear window. Her golden hair framed her face like a halo.

What beautiful hair! I thought. *I'd love to have curly hair, instead of brown pigtails.* I smiled and waved to her. She waved back. "Aunt Lydia," I said, "Mom told me Aunt Hannah wanted to make a Moravian dress for a girl named Charity. Is that the girl who needs the outfit?"

Aunt Lydia nodded. "Charity's playing the violin in the children's Easter program. All the girls except Charity have Moravian outfits to wear in the performance. Charity's mother died three years ago," Aunt Lydia explained, walking toward her bike. "Since Aunt Hannah and Uncle Luke don't have children, Aunt Hannah has taken Charity under her wing, makes most of her clothes, and gives her music and needlepoint lessons. Aunt Hannah says Charity has a gift for music. Charity was ill when she was little and has to wear leg braces and use crutches. Most of her schoolmates either shun or tease her. One particular girl, Cassandra, encourages the other kids to taunt Charity."

"That's cruel!" I stamped my foot and frowned. "I'd love to meet Charity. She needs a friend. Could we invite her to a tea party?"

"Charity is sensitive, quiet, and shy. She might refuse our invitation. However, I'll call Grandmother from the store and see if she can arrange for Charity and Aunt Hannah to have tea with us this evening." Aunt Lydia climbed on her bike. "We should leave now, Mimi. It's getting late."

I bent over to stroke Lilly's forelock. "Everything will be all right, Lilly," I whispered. "You'll have to stay tied to this tree, all by yourself, until Grandpa and Mr. Jason bring the trailer to take you to our farm." Lilly lifted her head and brayed softly. "You're going to have a warm stall, dry blankets, and good donkey food." I picked up Mom-Cat and walked reluctantly to my bike. "I'll come and see you, Lilly, as soon as we get home."

"Hop on your bike," Aunt Lydia said. "Instead of following the main road to town, we'll take a short cut. After we ride through the covered wooden bridge and pass the waterwheel, we'll turn left onto a graveled road. That road goes straight to town." I set Mom-Cat into the bike's basket and followed Aunt Lydia. Fifteen minutes later we arrived at her shop.

While I parked the bikes at the back of the building, Aunt Lydia unlocked the front door and switched on the lights. Then she turned the large "Closed" sign hanging on the front door to read "Open."

I put Patience on a stool by the shop's large front window where she could see everyone coming in and out the door. Mom-Cat, happy to be out of the bike basket, scampered to the back of the shop to search for a soft, secluded spot to take a nap. After finding a bundle of yarn piled next to an old spinning wheel, she curled up on top of it and purred contentedly. *I hope Lilly isn't hurt*, I thought as Aunt Lydia and I changed into our dresses in the back room and slipped on our aprons. *If Lilly is injured, Grandpa will know what to do.*

Later, Aunt Lydia showed me how to stock the shop's shelves with colorful bolts of cloth, rolls of ribbon, delicate lace, spools of thread, needles and pins, patterns, and skeins of yarn. She knew the name of every person who came into the shop. The day flew by and at exactly four o'clock we turned the sign in the front door over to read "Closed." Aunt Lydia locked the doors, and we climbed on our bikes and pedaled home.

Grandmother and Mrs. Jason were in the backyard taking the clean laundry off the clothesline when Aunt Lydia and I rode our bikes into the driveway. After we parked our bikes in the garage, I lifted Patience and Mom-Cat from the bike basket. I put Mom-Cat on the ground but carried Patience as Aunt Lydia and I dashed to the barn to see Lilly. Mom-Cat tagged along, walking with a stately manner.

Grandpa looked up from filling the horses' feed buckets when we entered the barn. "Hello, Mimi and Lydia," he said. "You'll be happy to hear Lilly doesn't have any injuries. All she needs is rest, good food, and lots of love. I think she misses Mr. and Mrs. Moses." Grandpa grinned and closed the door of the feed box. "After we got Lilly settled in her stall, Grandmother and I drove to the hospital to visit Mr. Moses. He wanted me to thank you, Aunt Lydia, Mr. Timothy, and Charity for rescuing Lilly. After he and I talked about his situation, we both agreed that it would be best for Lilly to stay at our farm until he's discharged from the hospital." Grandpa paused. "Then, Mr. Jason and I went over to Mr. Moses' farm and got Lilly's tack, blankets, sidesaddle, and two-wheeled open cart."

"Hurray!" I shouted. "Thank you, Grandpa."

"Mimi, I'll get a grooming kit from the tack room," Aunt Lydia said, "and show you how to groom Lilly. It's one of the best ways I know of bonding with a horse," she paused and added with a laugh, "or a donkey."

I tiptoed into Lilly's stall. She was lying on the straw-covered floor. "Lilly, I know you're homesick and lonesome, but everybody at Grandpa's farm loves you," I whispered, bending down on my knees and gently stroking her neck. "Look, I brought Mom-Cat to keep you company and Patience to meet you." Lilly lifted her head and brayed softly. Mom-Cat meowed, stretched lazily, and curled up in the soft straw next to Lilly.

When Aunt Lydia returned with the brushes, we coaxed Lilly to stand up. Then Aunt Lydia taught me how to groom Lilly. By the time we were finished, it was suppertime. "I'll be back later, Lilly," I said. I kissed her on the forehead. Then carrying Patience, I hurried to the house with Aunt Lydia. Chicken stew simmered on the kitchen stove and cheese biscuits and spicy molasses gingerbread were cooling on the counter.

Right after supper, I got my tap shoes out of my suitcase and went out to the barn with Grandpa to practice my dance routine. Grandpa laid a raised wooden platform on the floor in front of Lilly's stall to use for dancing. "If you need anything, Mimi, just holler. I'll be in the livery stable," Grandpa said. "I want to see if Lilly's cart needs to be repaired."

"Okay, Grandpa," I said. After he left, I went into Lilly's stall. She was lying down with her eyes closed. When I called her name she opened her eyes, lifted her head, and wiggled her big ears. The little lamb, Mom-Cat, and Pretzel were nestled on the straw covered floor next to her.

"Lilly, you're going to get stronger every day!" I said, gently stroking her head. "Look! You have two other friends." I petted the lamb. She felt like a warm, cuddly wool blanket. "While I'm practicing I'll think up a name for the lamb." I changed into my tap shoes, stepped onto the platform, and started dancing. "One, two, three! Brush, back, down!" I sang as I clapped my hands, danced back and forth, and twirled in circles.

Suddenly, I stopped singing and dancing. Lilly was standing up and staring intently at me. Mom-Cat, perched on Lilly's back, was grinning from ear to ear. Pretzel, Crystal, and the lamb were sitting by the stall door gazing at me with wide eyes. Lilly shook her head up and down and brayed loudly, "hee-haw, hee-haw." She had the biggest, whitest teeth I had ever seen.

"Mimi, it's time for tea." Aunt Lydia poked her head in the barn. "We have guests. Aunt Hannah, Uncle Luke, Mr. Timothy, and Charity came for tea. Come up to the house and join us!"

"Hurray!" I yelled. "I'll be right there, Aunt Lydia." I hopped off the wooden platform, wrapped my arms around Lilly's neck, and hugged her. "I'm glad you're smiling and have a sense of humor. Now I know why Mr. and Mrs. Moses named you Lilly. Your teeth are as pearly white as Grandmother's Easter lily." I lifted Mom-Cat from Lilly's back to the floor and changed my shoes. "Your name," I said, carrying the lamb back to her mother in the sheep pen next to the cows, "is Cuddly-Bell." I walked to the door, stopped, and turned. "Good night, everyone." Then I skipped and sang all the way to the farmhouse. Mom-Cat trailed behind me.

Aunt Lydia was arranging warm blueberry scones and cherry tarts on a three-tiered silver tray when I entered the kitchen. "What can I do to help?" I asked. I put my tap shoes in the closet then washed and dried my hands.

Aunt Lydia handed me a stack of white linen napkins and a bowl of fresh whipped cream. "If you'd like, you can carry the napkins and cream into the sitting room. Grandmother and Aunt Hannah agreed it was a wonderful idea to have Charity come for tea. Charity's looking forward to meeting you. She has a physical therapy appointment tomorrow morning. Mr. Timothy said she could only stay for about a half an hour." Aunt Lydia picked up the dessert tray. "Now let's go into the sitting room and have a tea party."

Grandmother's kind smile and Aunt Hannah's hearty laughter welcomed us as we entered the room. Aunt Hannah was round, short, jolly, and wore her dark hair styled like a doughnut on top of her head. She was seated beside Grandmother on the sofa. Charity was sitting in Grandpa's big chair, resting her head against his green velvet pillows. *She looks like the angel in the paintings hanging in the Angel Room,* I thought. Her wooden crutches lay on the large leather footstool in front of the chair.

After Aunt Lydia introduced me to Charity, she served the desserts. I gave everyone a napkin. Grandmother poured tea for the ladies, big mugs of coffee for Grandpa, Uncle Luke, and Mr. Timothy, and hot chocolate for Charity and me. The men carried their coffee and sweets to the parlor. They wanted to play chess and listen to the radio. Grandmother and Aunt Hannah took their tea to the sewing room to work on the blue and white star quilt they were making for the Moravian Alaska missions.

"Charity, did you get to your doctor's appointment on time?" Aunt Lydia asked. She sat down in the wingback chair that was in the corner between the window and the bookshelf and sipped her tea.

"Oh, yes. Thank you," Charity said softly, spreading her napkin over her lap. "How's Lilly?"

"Lilly's fine," I answered. "She's staying at our farm until Mr. Moses is discharged from the hospital."

"I thought she might have hurt her legs." Charity blushed and looked down at her braces. "I love animals. Mark, my big brother, and I don't have any pets. Because of the war, we had to move to Lititz. I'm going to ask my Dad if I can have a kitten." She nibbled daintily on her scone.

"The war forced our family to move to Bethlehem," I said. "My dog is in the K-9 Corps. Sometimes Mr. Sampson, our mailman, lets his cat, Mom-Cat, visit us." Suddenly

I had an idea. "Excuse me," I said. "I'll be right back." I put my teacup and saucer on the end table, dabbed my lips with the napkin, and dashed to the kitchen to get Mom-Cat and Pretzel. Those two were sleeping on Grandmother's rocking chair. With the cats in my arms I raced back to the sitting room. "Charity, this gray and white striped tabby is Mom-Cat." I set Mom-Cat on the footstool in front of Charity's chair. "Mom-Cat thinks she's a royal queen." Mom-Cat, thrilled by the attention, assumed a queenly pose and purred loudly.

"She's adorable," Charity said. "What's the name of the brown cat?"

"Grandpa calls her Pretzel because she acts like a contortionist in a circus when she stretches and twists up like a pretzel to sleep." I put Pretzel on the floor. Immediately, she stretched and coiled into a round fuzzy ball. We laughed at how ridiculous the cats appeared.

After we finished our tea, Aunt Lydia rose from her chair. "Girls, I have a surprise for you." Smiling widely, she reached behind her chair to retrieve two gaily-wrapped boxes, one round and the other square, both tied with silver ribbons. Aunt Lydia handed the round box to Charity and the square one to me.

"Thank you, Aunt Lydia," I said politely. "Since Charity is our guest, she can open her present first."

Charity slowly untied the bow and took the lid off the box. "Ooh!" she gasped. Blushing, she lifted out a straw brimmed Easter bonnet, sky blue dress with a pink satin sash and a cluster of pink satin rosebuds at the neck and hemline, and a pair of white gloves. "Thank you. This dress is beautiful. Blue is my favorite color." Her eyes were misty as she stroked the dress with shaking fingers, folded, and put it back in the box.

Aunt Lydia smiled at Charity and turned toward me. "Mimi, you're next."

I quickly untied the ribbon and opened the box. Wrapped in tissue paper was a black riding hat, white blouse with tie, tan jodhpurs, leather gloves, and a fitted, scarlet riding jacket with shiny gold buttons. "Hurray!" I jumped from my chair and hugged Aunt Lydia. "I've dreamed of a riding outfit exactly like this."

"Grandmother, Aunt Hannah, and Mrs. Jason made all the clothes," Aunt Lydia said. "They've been sewing for months. I hid the boxes behind this chair last week waiting for the ideal time to give them to you. I do hope everything is the right size." She sighed. "I ordered the hats and gloves from a mail order catalog."

I put on the jacket, plopped the hat on my head, and slipped on the gloves. "I'm off to the sewing room," I said, "to thank Grandmother and Aunt Hannah." I turned and darted toward the door. In my excitement, the hat's visor slipped down over my eyes. I tripped over the footstool in front of Charity's chair. **BANG!** Charity's crutches crashed to the floor. Shocked, Mom-Cat meowed and bounded off the stool. "Oh! I'm sorry, Charity and

Mom-Cat." I stooped, petted Mom-Cat, picked up Charity's crutches, and leaned them against the side of the sofa.

"Mimi, please thank your Grandmother and Aunt Hannah for me," Charity said as I flew out the door.

A few minutes later, when I returned, Charity had on her hat and coat.

"It's time for Charity to leave," Aunt Lydia said. "Mr. Timothy took Charity's box of clothes out to their car." She got up from her seat. "While you were in the sewing room, I told Charity about our plan to design and sew an Easter banner for the town's parade. She volunteered to help you."

"My Dad said he'd drive me to and from the farm every evening until Easter," Charity said, "for tea and to sew on the banner." She slipped a crutch under each arm and struggled to her feet. Her cheeks turned beet red from the effort, but she didn't utter a sound. Using her crutches for support, she hobbled from the sitting room down the carpeted hallway to the kitchen. Aunt Lydia walked in front guiding her, and I followed.

"Thank you for offering to help make the banner," I said when we were in the kitchen. "Good-bye, Charity."

"I'm glad I met you and Mom-Cat and Pretzel," Charity said as Mr. Timothy assisted her out the door to the car. "The tea party was fun."

After they left, I said goodnight to everyone and then bounced up the stairs clutching my riding outfit close to my heart. Later, Grandmother came up to hear my prayers. We sang some of my favorite songs and hymns as she closed the drapes and smoothed my covers. Exhausted, happy, and grateful for my riding outfit and new friends, I fell asleep as soon as my head touched the pillow with Patience and teddy bear in my arms and Mom-Cat curled up on the side of the bed.

CHAPTER FOUR

My First Riding Lesson

The following day, when Aunt Lydia and I came home from her yard goods shop, all the doors and windows in the farmhouse were wide open, and the parlor tapestry drapes and wool carpets were hanging on the backyard clothesline. "Grandmother and Mrs. Jason have started the annual spring housecleaning," Aunt Lydia said as we parked our bikes by the porch steps. "They'll be bustling from the cellar to the attic dusting, cleaning, and scouring everything in sight until Good Friday." She laughed.

"Come in and have some warm apple fritters or a fresh-baked raisin cinnamon roll," Grandmother called to us from the kitchen door. "The rolls are in the breadbox and the fritters are on a platter on the kitchen table. The tea kettle's boiling on the stove." Then shouldering the dust mop, broom, feather duster, and a basket of cleaning supplies, she turned and marched down the hall toward the parlor, humming one of her favorite hymns.

"I don't think a speck of dust," Aunt Lydia said as we entered the kitchen, "could escape from Grandmother's scrutinizing eyes." We hung our coats in the closet.

I had a raisin cinnamon roll, an apple fritter, and a tall glass of cold milk. That was the most delicious snack I ever had! When Aunt Lydia and I finished, we rushed upstairs to change into our flannel shirts and jodhpurs. Aunt Lydia loaned me a pair of her shiny black-leather riding boots. They were too big. I solved that problem by putting on an extra pair of wool socks.

"Mimi, I'll race you to the barn," Aunt Lydia said as we hurried from the kitchen and down the porch steps. We both took off across the lawn. Laughing, we entered the barn at the same time. Graceful Lady gave a welcoming whinny, and Lilly wiggled her ears and brayed loudly.

"I'm glad you're feeling better," I said, rubbing Lilly's neck. Nearby, Crystal, Mom-Cat, Pretzel, and Cuddly-Bell lay napping on a soft mound of hay. "Wake up, sleepy heads! Aunt Lydia and I are going to groom Graceful Lady and Lilly. Then we'll tack up Graceful Lady. You're all invited to watch my first riding lesson."

I felt jittery as Aunt Lydia and I led Graceful Lady from the barn to the wooden mounting

block at the arena's entrance gate. Thrilled but nervous, I climbed the mounting block's stairs and slid onto Graceful Lady's saddle. *Another one of my dreams is coming true,* I thought. *I'm determined to learn to ride, but I never imagined an English saddle would be this small or I'd be sitting so high off the ground. I hope I don't get dizzy and fall.* My hands trembled as I pulled on my leather gloves.

Aunt Lydia adjusted the stirrups and showed me how to hold the reins. "Mimi, I want you to focus on keeping your balance, giving commands, and steering," she said. "Graceful Lady is a calm, smooth-gaited walker, and an experienced show horse. Like Mom-Cat, she's always the perfect lady. She loves being in the spotlight, playing to the crowd, and being in control." Then Aunt Lydia took hold of the lead rope and began leading Graceful Lady around the ring. I was concentrating so hard I lost track of time.

"We've been practicing for forty-five minutes," Aunt Lydia said. "That's enough work for today. Tomorrow you can ride Graceful Lady, and I'll ride along side you on Freedom. Don't worry. Graceful Lady will be alert and respond to any commands you give her."

"Let's stop in front of the mounting block by the gate. I want to dismount all by myself." My legs felt wobbly as I climbed out of the saddle. "Ooh!" I cried and stumbled down the steps. "I'm all right, Aunt Lydia. My legs are stiff." I grabbed onto the fence post.

"The more you ride, the more confident and relaxed you'll be," Aunt Lydia said, patting my back. "For your first time on a horse you did a great job. You'll look fabulous leading the parade in your scarlet jacket and carrying the banner." I glowed with pride as we walked Graceful Lady back to her stall.

Aunt Lydia and I were putting Graceful Lady's saddle and bridle in the tack room when Grandpa strolled into the barn. "Supper's ready. Take your time. Grandmother is keeping dinner in the warming oven until you're ready to join us."

We had just finished our scrumptious supper of sauerbraten, mashed potatoes and gravy, and sourdough biscuits when Charity, Mr. Timothy, Aunt Hannah, and Uncle Luke arrived. Grandpa met them at the front door and ushered them into the sitting room. Aunt Lydia made coffee, tea, and hot chocolate. Grandmother took the shoo-fly pie from her pie cupboard and set it and a bowl of sweet whipped cream on her teacart. "I'll put the silver tea set, cups, and dishes on the teacart," I offered. "Then I'll get my Moravian outfit."

"Thank you, Mimi," Grandmother said. "Aunt Hannah and I want to begin sewing on Charity's Moravian dress this evening." She looked up from slicing the pie. "I'm glad you and Charity are becoming friends. It breaks Grandpa's and my heart to see the way some of the children mock and ridicule her."

I carefully placed the tea set and china on the cart. Then I ran down the hall and up the stairs to the Angel Room. I took my Moravian outfit from my suitcase and picked up Patience and my teddy bear from off the bed. I glanced at Mom-Cat sleeping in her basket. "Mom-Cat, I'm worried about you. I've never seen you take so many naps." I frowned. "Uncle Luke's a doctor. I'm taking you downstairs and asking him to look at you."

When I entered the kitchen, Grandpa was setting up the chessboard on the kitchen table. "Grandpa, where's everybody?" My eyes circled the room.

"Aunt Lydia and Grandmother are in the sitting room with Charity and Aunt Hannah," Grandpa said. He looked up from his chess pieces on the board. "Mr. Jason's in the barn, and Uncle Luke left to make a house call for one of his patients. Since it started raining and there is a strong wind, Mr. Timothy went with him."

"Grandpa, do you think Uncle Luke has time to examine Mom-Cat? She's sleeping more than usual." I wrinkled my forehead. "I don't know if she's ill, home-sick, or lazy. "

"I'm sure Uncle Luke won't mind examining Mom-Cat. He doesn't go anywhere without his stethoscope and black-leather medical bag." Grandpa winked at me and grinned.

"Thank you, Grandpa." I set Mom-Cat on the cushion next to Pretzel in Grandmother's rocking chair and rushed from the kitchen to the sitting room.

Grandmother was serving tea and dishing up the shoo-fly pie. Each slice, covered with a peak of whipped cream, looked like a snow-capped mountain. Aunt Hannah and Charity sat together on the leather sofa facing a blazing, crackling fire in the fireplace. Charity's wooden crutches leaned against the sofa. An artist's easel stood in the center of the room. A pencil box, crayons, and paints were lying on the nearby table.

"Hello," I said, handing Aunt Hannah all the pieces to my Moravian outfit. Aunt Hannah flashed me a bright smile. Charity looked up and nodded shyly. "Charity, I'd like you to meet my doll, Patience, and my teddy bear. My bear lost some of his fur. Mom and I sewed patches over his bald spots." I put Patience and my teddy bear in the children's low rocker by the fireplace. "My Mom made Patience. She's dressed in a Moravian outfit."

"Your teddy bear is cute." Charity smiled. "Patience is pretty."

"Charity, Grandmother and Aunt Hannah are making your Moravian outfit exactly like mine and the outfit Patience is wearing," I said, sitting down in the chair next to the sofa. "We both get red ribbons to lace our jackets and for the ties of our caps."

"A long time ago," Grandmother explained, "the Moravian women and girls dressed alike. However, the ribbons they used to lace their jackets and to tie their caps were different colors. All the girls wore bright red ribbons, the married ladies wore blue ribbons, the unmarried ladies wore pink ribbons, and the widows white ribbons. Their long full skirts, called petticoats, and jackets were often made from chocolate-brown wool. The long waist-length aprons, shifts, neckerchiefs, and caps were sewn from white linen." She rose from her chair and walked toward the door. "If you'll excuse us, Aunt Hannah and I are taking our tea to the sewing room. We need to begin making Charity's outfit."

"Mimi, since Charity is helping you make the banner," Aunt Lydia said, "I'll work on Charity's outfit. You can use the drawing easel and pencils and paints on the table to design the banner. Tomorrow, we'll get the sewing supplies for your project at the shop." She stood by my side for a moment then followed Grandmother and Aunt Hannah out of the room. "If you need anything please let me know."

Then Charity and I were alone. We both sat quietly eating our pie. I stared down at the marshmallow melting in my cup of hot chocolate. I couldn't think of a thing to say.

All of a sudden, I heard the kitchen door slam and Uncle Luke's voice. Pretzel and Mom-Cat burst into the sitting room! Mom-Cat leaped onto Charity's lap. With a loud meow, Pretzel dived onto mine.

"Oooh!" Charity shrieked. She flung her arms open. Her teacup, saucer, and spoon crashed to the floor, landing on Grandmother's braided wool rug.

"Mom-Cat and Pretzel, you scared Charity," I said. I lifted Pretzel from off my lap, put her on the floor, and turned toward Charity. "I've never seen Mom-Cat act so rudely. The wind slamming the door shut and Uncle Luke's loud voice must have startled them." I bent down on my hands and knees, picked up the dishes, and put them on the teacart. "It's all right. Nothing broke."

"I'm glad my cup and plate were empty," Charity murmured. "The chocolate and pie would've stained the rug."

"Excuse me, Charity. I'm taking these cats back to the kitchen." I lifted Mom-Cat from Charity's lap, picked up Pretzel, and marched toward the sitting room door. "There's a horse magazine and horse picture books on the table by your chair. I'll be right back."

When I returned, Charity was leafing through the magazine. She quickly closed it and put it on the table. "Mimi, I'm not good at talking," she apologized, clasping her hands. "When I talk to people, I feel like they're staring at my legs and there's a big lump in my throat. But I'm patient and a good listener."

"It's hard for me to be patient," I said. I sat down in the chair by the bookcase. "Grandpa calls me a chatterbox, so we should get along fine."

"Most kids don't want to play with me because I use crutches," she confided. "Books are my friends. I love to read, sing, and play my violin. I'd like to be a teacher when I grow up. My big brother, Mark, wants to be a doctor like your Uncle Luke."

"Writing stories and reading are my favorite pastime. I'm going to be a nurse, write books, travel, and own an Arabian horse when I grew up," I said. "Aunt Lydia is giving me horseback riding lessons."

"I like to imagine I can walk and run without crutches and ride horseback." Charity sighed, looked down at her legs, and then up at me. "Sometimes the kids laugh and call me four legs," she said with a quivering voice.

"That's mean!" I jumped from my chair and put my hands on my hips. "Aunt Lydia said a girl named Cassandra teases you more than the others."

"Cassandra is the president of the children's county riding club. She has a Shetland pony and has won lots of gold trophies and blue ribbons in horse shows."

"Cassandra's also a big bully." I sat down on the sofa next to Charity. "I'm going to ask Aunt Lydia to talk to your Dad and Uncle Luke about letting you have riding lessons. Lilly would be perfect for you to ride. She's gentle and sure-footed."

"I'd love to ride Lilly," Charity said. "If I could ride, the kids might ask me to join their riding club."

"Look how much we're alike," I said, listing our similarities. "We're both bookworms, have good imaginations, older brothers, love tea parties, want horseback riding lessons, and have had to move because of the war." I leaned toward Charity and put my arm around her shoulder. "Let's be friends and pretend to be sisters."

"Oh! I've always wanted a true friend," Charity said, "and a big sister."

"Wonderful! We'll be true, loyal friends and sisters, forever." I got up from the sofa and opened the pencil box. "Now, that's settled. Let's design our banner." I walked over to the front of the easel. "We need to decide on a color, symbol, and motto." For several minutes I stood staring at the blank paper attached to the easel.

"We could make a blue banner," Charity said in a timid voice, wringing her hands nervously in her lap.

"That's a great idea! We'll make it as blue as Aunt Lydia's sapphire engagement ring," I said. "For our symbol, I'll draw an empty brown cross in the middle of the banner and outline it in bright yellow." I picked up a pencil and started sketching.

"An empty cross," Charity said, "is the perfect symbol for Easter."

"Since the war began, my favorite phrase is 'Love One Another,'" I said. "How does that sound for a motto?"

"I like it because it's something everyone can do." Charity slowly pushed herself up from the sofa. Using her crutches, she limped over to the easel.

"I'll print the words in big letters around the cross so they're easy to read."

"Can you draw green palm branches in each corner of the banner?" Charity asked.

I nodded. "Tomorrow, I'll get the blue material, colored felt, and thread at the shop. Aunt

Lydia was planning to stop at Aunt Hannah's house on our way home. I'll ask Aunt Hannah to help me cut out the banner and hem it on her sewing machine. In the evening you and I can cut out the cross, palm branches, and letters from the felt and stitch them onto the banner," I said as I continued drawing. Ten minutes later I looked up from the easel and turned toward Charity. "I'm finished." I put the pencils back in the box. "How does it look?"

"It's beautiful," Charity said. She smiled. "I love the bright colors."

"Ladies, pardon me for interrupting," Grandpa said, standing in the sitting room doorway. "Uncle Luke had to hurry off again for an emergency at the hospital. Before he left he gave Mom-Cat a thorough examination." Grandpa paused and grinned broadly. "The findings from Uncle Luke's exam indicate Mom-Cat's going to have kittens!"

"Kittens!" I shouted. Shocked, I dropped the pencil box. "When? How many?"

"Uncle Luke says Mom-Cat's kittens are probably due in about two weeks," Grandpa replied, "and she'll have about five to seven."

"In two weeks," I echoed, wiping my forehead. "What else did Uncle Luke say?"

"Now, don't worry, honey. Uncle Luke said Mom-Cat would be fine. She's an experienced mother." Grandpa walked over to me and gave me a hug. "Since Mom-Cat likes to visit Lilly in the barn, I made a bed for her from one of Grandmother's old clothes baskets, lined it with a soft purple blanket, and put it in Lilly's stall."

"Mimi, Mr. Timothy has his car ready to take Charity and Aunt Hannah home," Aunt Lydia called from the hallway. "Uncle Luke is still at the hospital." She walked into the sitting room carrying Charity's coat and hat as the grandfather clock in the parlor chimed half past eight.

After Charity and Aunt Hannah left, I showed everyone the drawing of our banner.

"Good work!" Grandpa said. Grandmother and Aunt Lydia nodded and smiled approvingly.

"Mimi, I need to lock the barn door," Grandpa said. "It stopped raining, but we might have another storm tonight. I'll put the easel away later. Would you like to walk to the barn with me?"

"Oh, yes, Grandpa." I picked up the scattered pencils from off the floor and ran to get my jacket and hat.

Darkness gathered around the farm as Grandpa and I walked to the barn, but I felt safe and secure with my hand in Grandpa's, and the light from the kerosene lantern guiding our steps along the gravel path. The cold evening air nipped my nose and cheeks. I was glad I was wearing my hat and jacket.

"Grandpa, I love staying at the farm. Aunt Lydia's teaching me to ride, and I've found new friends: Charity, Lilly, and the little lamb. Charity and I are pretending we're sisters."

"Good," Grandpa said. "Charity's a sweet girl. She may look weak and frail, but she possesses a strong faith and character. In spite of all Charity's been through, she's not bitter. She is loving and gentle."

"Why do you think some of the kids tease and ignore her?" I asked.

"Well, Mimi, everyone wants to be accepted and loved," Grandpa replied gravely. "But, sometimes fear or simply being unaware of another's physical challenges can cause people to be thoughtless or unkind to those who are different or disabled."

"That's why Charity and I chose 'Love One Another' for the banner's motto," I said earnestly. I held the lantern over my head while Grandpa latched the barn door. "Grandpa, do you have a flag pole I can use for the banner?" We turned and walked back toward the house.

"There's a brand new pole in the hayloft," Grandpa said. "I'll get it down for you next week. Meanwhile, there's an old one in the garage you can use. By the way, I visited Mr. Moses at the hospital today. I told him Lilly was thriving from your good care. Mr. Moses is concerned about Lilly getting enough exercise. He wondered if you'd like to ride her for about an hour every day. He said to tell you she's not as smooth a walker as Graceful Lady." Grandpa laughed heartily. "On the other hand, you're not sitting as high off the ground as you are on a horse."

"Tell Mr. Moses thank you. I'd be happy to ride Lilly." I handed Grandpa the lantern as we entered the warm kitchen. "Now all I have to do is sew the banner, learn to ride, and win a trophy. Then my Easter will be marvelous."

"All that in less than two weeks! However, with your enthusiasm and persistence I'm sure you'll get everything done." Grandpa looked down at me, smiled, and turned off the lantern. He put his arm around my shoulders and drew me close. "Good night, honey. I'm going into the sitting room to read the paper and listen to the late news on the radio."

Grandmother, wrapped in a pink wool shawl, was sitting in her rocking chair next to the stove knitting. Aunt Lydia, curled up in a kitchen chair, was writing a letter to Uncle Jim. She wrote to him every day. On the kitchen table, by her box of airmail stationery and bottle of ink, stood a framed picture of Uncle Jim in his Army uniform.

I hung my hat and jacket on the coat rack by the door. "Charity would love to have riding lessons," I said, turning to Aunt Lydia. "Do you think her legs are strong enough to ride Lilly?"

Aunt Lydia stopped writing, looked up, and smiled. "We'll have to ask Uncle Luke," she said. "I'd like to teach Charity to ride. She'd have fun, and it would build her confidence. I'll talk with her Dad and Uncle Luke and explain that I have a special loop-handled saddle designed for children and a child's sidesaddle that she could use to ride Lilly."

"Thank you, Aunt Lydia!" I hugged her.

"Mimi, next week is Holy Week," Grandmother said. "Every day will be filled with spring-cleaning, sewing, preparations for Easter, and church in the evenings."

"My shop will be closed all day Maundy Thursday, Good Friday, the Great Sabbath, and Easter Sunday," Aunt Lydia added.

After I bade Grandmother and Aunt Lydia goodnight, I picked up Mom-Cat, who was sleeping peacefully next to Pretzel on the crocheted rag rug in front of the stove. Cradling her in my arms, I carried her upstairs to the Angel Room. "I'm sorry, Mom-Cat," I said. "You can't go to Aunt Lydia's shop until your kittens are born." I laid her tenderly in her basket by my bed and covered her up.

Then I knelt by the window and gazed up at the shining moon and twinkling stars. On Grandpa's farm there weren't any street lamps, bright lights from the steel company, or city to spoil the beauty of the night sky.

I folded my hands and said my prayers. Tired, I got up, closed the drapes, and put on my nightgown. "Good night, Mom-Cat," I whispered, crawling into bed. "I love you." Mom-Cat replied with a sleepy meow.

Chapter Five

Rise And Shine

My days at the farm were happy and busy and the days flew by quickly. Every morning Grandpa rang the large bell in the backyard and cried "rise and shine" to wake anyone who dared oversleep. Then Grandpa and Mr. Jason continued their farm chores.

Before breakfast, I practiced my tap dancing lessons in the barn in front of Lilly's stall, while Grandpa and Mr. Jason finished milking the cows. Grandmother served breakfast at seven o'clock. Immediately after breakfast, Grandpa read the Scriptures and prayer from the *Moravian Daily Texts Book*. By nine o'clock Aunt Lydia and I had her shop open and were ready to welcome any ladies who needed sewing, knitting, or crocheting items. Grandmother always had a yummy snack waiting for us when we came home.

The best part of my day was my riding lesson. It lasted until suppertime. Grandmother, known for her good cooking skills and hospitality, kept an empty chair and place setting at the supper table for any unexpected visitor.

Having tea and dessert every evening at the farm was a family tradition. Grandmother always used her silver tea set and delicate china teacups and served the tea by candlelight on a low, lace-covered table in front of the fireplace in the sitting room.

Bookcases, as tall as the ceiling, lined two walls of this cozy room. Their shelves bulged with Grandmother's collection of Moravian books, hymnals, and Bibles. Grandmother was an ardent collector of Bibles and refused to throw away a Bible no matter how old, ripped, tattered, or worn.

I was glad that Mr. Timothy said Charity could join us every evening for tea and to sew on the banner. After tea, we'd gather around the piano and sing our favorite songs and hymns while Aunt Hannah played the piano. Then, while Grandmother, Aunt Hannah, and Aunt Lydia sewed on Charity's outfit, and Charity and I labored over the banner, I'd use my imagination to make up and tell stories. Sometimes my stories were so funny we'd get the giggles.

Although my bedtime was at nine o'clock, some nights after Mr. Timothy took Charity home, Grandmother would read her Moravian history books to me and let me stay up later.

It was hard to believe that tomorrow would be Palm Sunday and my first week at the farm was almost over.

CHAPTER SIX

Charity, Faith, and Hope

Palm Sunday morning arrived sunny, crisp, and breezy. I went to Charity's Sunday school class while Aunt Lydia, Grandpa, and Grandmother attended the adult Bible study. Charity and I wore our Sunday dresses, straw hats, white gloves, and took our Bibles. I noticed only a few kids talked to Charity. When our class was over, Charity's Sunday school teacher asked me to take part in the children's Easter program and wear my Moravian outfit.

During the church service, Charity and I sat in the first pew, close to the choir. We loved the organ music and to hear the choir sing. Grandmother, Aunt Lydia, and Grandpa stood by the front door and greeted the members of the congregation and visitors. Uncle Luke and Mr. Timothy were ushers.

"Mimi and Charity, I have good news!" Aunt Lydia said in a low voice after the service as we waited in the vestibule of the church for Grandmother, Grandpa, and Mr. Timothy. "Grandmother invited Charity, Mr. Timothy, Mark, Uncle Luke, and Aunt Hannah for lunch and supper." She smiled widely. "And Charity has permission from Uncle Luke and Mr. Timothy to have riding lessons."

"Thank you," I said. I wrapped my arms around Aunt Lydia's neck and gave her a big hug. Charity's face glowed with happiness and her blue eyes gleamed.

That afternoon, after we ate lunch, Aunt Lydia, Charity, and I went to the barn. Aunt Lydia bridled Lilly and Graceful Lady, and I showed Charity the little lamb, Cuddly-Bell, and the other horses grazing in the pasture. Later, Mr. Timothy, Mark, Uncle Luke, Mr. Jason, and Grandpa walked down from the house to the arena to watch our riding lessons. They sat with Charity on the wooden bench by the arena's gate while I rode Graceful Lady and practiced posting and trotting.

"Good work, Mimi," Aunt Lydia said, standing by the hitching post next to the gate. "By Fall you should be cantering." She untied Lilly's rope from the post. "Let's see how you do riding Lilly." After circling the arena one more time, I dismounted Graceful Lady by the hitching post, and Mr. Jason led her to the barn.

I didn't need assistance to climb onto Lilly's saddle. I felt she loved and wanted to please me as soon as I picked up the reins. When I was riding Graceful Lady, tall and dignified, she strutted around the ring. I worked hard to gain her trust and affection. Lilly, short and humble, had a plodding pace and eagerly obeyed my commands.

After I circled the arena twice, I dismounted Lilly and stroked her neck. "Good girl," I said. Lilly brayed and nuzzled my shoulder. "It's your turn," I called to Charity.

Charity rose from the bench and hobbled with her crutches to the center of the arena. "Mimi, I'm glad I can have riding lessons," she whispered in an anxious tone while Aunt Lydia exchanged Lilly's saddle for the special loop-handled saddle, "but my hands are shaking. I feel like there are butterflies in my stomach." She gave me her crutches and leaned against Lilly.

"I felt the same way. You'll be a great rider," I said reassuringly. "Lilly is calm and slow-paced."

Uncle Luke came forward and lifted Charity onto Lilly's saddle. "Steady, Lilly," I said. I patted her neck, and Uncle Luke adjusted the stirrups for Charity's legs.

Then Aunt Lydia showed Charity how to hold the reins. "Charity, the saddle has a front loop that you can grasp if you feel nervous," Aunt Lydia said. She took hold of Lilly's lead rope and began leading her around the arena. The rest of us leaned on the wooden fence railing and cheered and clapped.

Thirty minutes later, Grandpa lifted Charity from Lilly's saddle. "You were terrific," I shouted. I ran to give Charity her crutches. "I knew you could do it."

"I've never had so much fun in my whole life!" Charity exclaimed.

"We're all proud of you," Aunt Lydia said. "Learning to ride takes courage, patience, and practice. I have stacks of books on horsemanship you and Mimi are welcome to read. Let's walk Lilly to the barn. After we brush Graceful Lady and Lilly, we'll all help Grandmother peel potatoes for supper."

For the next three days, during our riding sessions, Charity rode Lilly and I practiced with Graceful Lady.

Every other minute Charity and I were together, we either sewed on the banner or read Aunt Lydia's equestrian books.

Now, it was Maundy Thursday and Easter would be here soon. Charity and I had our lessons in the morning because Aunt Lydia's shop was closed. It was gloomy, rainy, and cold but nothing could dampen our enthusiasm.

Afterwards, Charity and I went to the house for a cup of hot chocolate and apple strudel. Then we went back to sewing the banner. Aunt Lydia took her tea into the sewing room to help Grandmother and Aunt Hannah. By noon, Charity and I had sewn the last felt pieces on our banner. Proudly we folded the banner and put it in a box in the kitchen closet. Before Charity went home, Grandmother and Aunt Hannah presented Charity with her completed Moravian outfit, carefully wrapped in white tissue paper.

Later that day, Grandmother hosted an Easter tea for the church choir. Aunt Lydia and I decorated the parlor with bouquets of tulips, daffodils, and Easter lilies while Grandpa built a fire in the fireplace to take off the chill. I put on a clean white pinafore and helped Aunt Lydia greet the people at the front door and escort them to their seats. Grandmother served little tea sandwiches, plump blackberry scones topped with dollops of clotted cream and jam, and Moravian molasses cookies. All the ladies wore hats and gloves.

The grandfather clock in the parlor chimed five o'clock as the last guests said their farewells and Grandmother, Aunt Lydia, and I walked them to the front door. Exhausted, we collapsed on the sofa and nibbled on leftover scones.

"Oh, my! The evening service starts in less than two hours," Grandmother said, looking at the clock. "I'll need your help to tidy up the parlor. The carpet sweeper needs to be run and the dishes washed before we leave." She stood and hurried to get the sweeper from the closet. Laughing, Aunt Lydia and I got up from the sofa, and scrambled to stack the dirty dishes on the teacart and whisk them to the kitchen.

"I'll wash the dishes for you, Aunt Lydia," I offered. I filled the round, porcelain dishpan in the sink with hot soapy water and watched the soap bubbles bounce merrily on top of the water.

"Mimi, I don't know how to tell you this," Aunt Lydia said in a distraught voice, taking a dishtowel from the kitchen drawer. "The Easter parade has been canceled."

"Ooh! No," I gasped. Stunned, I gazed into Aunt Lydia's eyes. "Why?"

"Due to shortages caused by the war," Aunt Lydia said. "With the scarcity of items and the expense of decorations and floats, the group in charge of the parade decided to put the parade funds toward the War Effort." She sighed. "Grandmother and I didn't have the heart to tell you and Charity this morning."

I turned on the hot water spigot and picked up a teacup. Overwhelmed with despair I bent my head and stared at the dishpan. The soapy water overflowed from the pan. The bubbles burst like my dreams and ran swiftly down the drain.

I swallowed and took a deep breath. "Thank you for my riding outfit and lessons," I said. Slowly, I washed and rinsed the cup and turned off the water. I blinked and bit my bottom lip. I didn't want Aunt Lydia to see tears in my eyes.

"I'm sorry," Aunt Lydia said, putting her arm around my shoulder. "I'll finish doing the dishes. Grandpa is in the barn. You can share a plate of your favorite molasses cookies with him and ask him to get ready for church."

Silently, I dried my hands, took the plate of cookies off the table, and went out to the barn. I found Grandpa sitting at his workbench, whistling, and carving a pair of candlesticks. "Grandpa, it's time to get ready for the evening service," I said. "I brought you some cookies. I don't want any." I put the plate on his workbench and collapsed on the high wooden stool next to him. "Did you know the parade's been canceled because of the war?"

"Yes, honey." Grandpa stopped whittling and put his carving tools in his workbench drawer.

"I understand how important it is," I said softly, "for everyone to support the War Effort."

"But sometimes," Grandpa added, "it can be challenging." He looked thoughtful. "I know you had your heart set on leading the parade. The cancellation is a bitter disappointment for you and a lot of other children."

"You and Grandmother can have the banner. It will look beautiful hanging on the front porch."

"I wouldn't give that banner away or fret. It's only Maundy Thursday. Who knows what will happen by Easter." He got up from his stool and walked toward the door. "Remember, our church always has a special children's program after the early morning Easter service."

"Grandpa, would you please tell Aunt Lydia I'll be up to the house after I see if Lilly needs any food or water?"

"I would be happy to, Mimi," Grandpa said. "Don't linger long."

After Grandpa left, I filled Lilly's water bucket and food bag. Dejected, I sank onto a bale of hay. "I feel miserable," I said to Lilly, Mom-Cat, Pretzel, Crystal, and Cuddly-Bell, who had followed me into the stall. I bent my head and covered my eyes with my hands. Cuddly-Bell bleated softly. Mom-Cat and Pretzel meowed, Lilly brayed, and Crystal whined and lay down at my feet. *Everything's ruined,* I thought. *I worked hard to learn to ride, and Charity and I spent hours making the banner. All our effort was wasted. What will I tell Charity?*

Suddenly, I cringed. "Ooh, no!" I groaned. *How could I have been so selfish? For two weeks Charity helped me so my dream could come true. Yet, I never asked her if she dreamed of being in the parade. I hoped our motto would inspire people to be kind and caring, but I've been so involved with my dreams, I failed to think about others.* Overcome with shame, I shook my head sorrowfully. *I've learned our motto is easier to say than do. From this instant,* I vowed, *I'm turning those words into action. I'll start by getting the pole down from the hayloft for Grandpa. It will save him some work.* I stood and marched toward the back of the barn to the ladder leading to the loft. *Tomorrow morning, I'll surprise Grandpa and Grandmother by hanging the banner on their porch and apologize to Charity.*

Slowly, I climbed the up the ladder's narrow steps. When I reached the top and stepped onto the loft's creaky wooden floor, Mom-Cat and Pretzel welcomed me with loud meows.

They had found a faster route by jumping and climbing on storage boxes and stacks of hay. My eyes quickly darted around the loft. Cobwebs hung from the rafters and wooden crates were stacked against two walls. A spinning wheel, a wooden wash tub and scrub board, a butter churn, and an old cherry wood dressing table with a cracked mirror and matching chair were shoved against the far wall. The flagpole stood in the corner behind the dressing table. I walked to the table, stood on my tiptoes, and stretched to reach the pole. I grabbed it and spun around.

BANG! The pole hit the dressing table. Checking to see if I had scratched it, I saw the name *"Catherine Marie Noble"* engraved on a brass plate on the center drawer. Below the nameplate was a small keyhole. All of a sudden, it flashed into my thoughts, *Catherine Marie Noble was my great-grandmother's name. This must have been her dressing table.* Curious, I leaned the pole against the wall, stooped, and pulled on the brass knob. The drawer wouldn't budge. It was locked. Quickly, I searched the other four drawers for a key. They were all empty except the bottom right one. Built into the back of that drawer was a small secret compartment with a sliding door. Cautiously, I slid the door open and peered inside. To my amazement, there were two rusty keys on a round key ring. I picked up the key ring, closed my eyes, and imagined I could see my great-grandmother dressed in an old-fashioned gown hiding the keys in this secret compartment.

"Mimi," Aunt Lydia called from below, "it's time to leave for the evening service. Where are you?"

"Oh!" Startled, my eyes flew open. The keys plunged to the floor. Mom-Cat and Pretzel leaped on the table. Dust and straw flew everywhere.

"I'm up in the hayloft," I called down to her, "getting the flagpole for Grandpa." I quickly picked up the keys and put them back in the secret compartment.

"Please come down!" Aunt Lydia said. "Grandmother and Grandpa are in the car waiting for us. Hurry, or we'll be late for church. Leave the pole in the loft. We can get it tomorrow."

I closed the drawer and scurried down the ladder. "I'm sorry, Aunt Lydia," I apologized. I felt miserable. *In less than five minutes,* I thought, *I destroyed my good intentions.*

"Mimi, you know how Grandmother and Grandpa are about being punctual for church," Aunt Lydia said. She smiled. "I brought your coat, hat, and Bible." She vigorously brushed bits of straw from my hair and dress. Then she slipped her hand through my arm and we ran to Grandpa's car, idling in the driveway.

We were the last ones to enter the church. Aunt Hannah was playing the organ, but the service hadn't started. I breathed a sigh of relief as we filed into the last empty pew in the back of the church. Mr. Timothy, Charity, and Mark were sitting two rows in front of us.

They left as soon as the service was over. Charity's eyes met mine, and we both smiled as she walked down the aisle toward the vestibule.

Shortly after we got home from church, the kitchen wall telephone rang. Aunt Lydia, always waiting for a call from Uncle Jim or one of his military friends, dashed to answer it.

Grandpa and I went into the sitting room to play records on the Victrola. While Grandpa sorted a stack of records, I curled up in a chair and looked at one of Aunt Lydia's horse magazines.

Suddenly, Aunt Lydia burst into the room. "That call was from Aunt Hannah. Grandmother is on the phone talking with her. Aunt Hannah called to say since the Easter parade has been canceled, some parents from church want to organize an Easter family picnic. For the entertainment they're having a children's story contest. She invited Grandmother to the planning meeting tomorrow morning at her home."

"A story contest!" I echoed. "Hurray!" I sprang to my feet and clapped my hands.

"According to Aunt Hannah, the biggest obstacle facing the committee," Aunt Lydia said, "is finding a suitable location to hold the event." She wrinkled her brow.

Then I had an idea. "Grandpa, could we hold the picnic and contest at your farm, and have a children's parade in the riding arena, and an egg hunt in the orchard?" I continued.

"The parade and story contest could be held before the picnic. Afterwards we could have the egg hunt." I paused and took a big breath. "Please, Grandpa."

"Grandmother and I have hosted parties and picnics at the farm," Grandpa said, shaking his head slowly, "but we've never had a children's parade, an egg hunt, or a storytelling contest."

"That's true," Aunt Lydia said. She walked straight across the room and stood at the back of my chair. "Just think how many happy children there will be if we hold the event here." She smiled. "Don't you agree having an Easter parade on the Great Sabbath at the farm would be fun for children and grown-ups?"

"Where would we put all the people?" Grandpa said thoughtfully, stroking his chin.

"We can borrow chairs and tables from the church," Aunt Lydia suggested, "and I'm sure people would offer to bring extra folding chairs. The tables and chairs could be set up in the backyard and meadow and around the riding arena."

"Grandpa, we could call our event an Easter Pageant," I said, "and ask each family to bring their favorite potluck dish to share at the picnic, colored eggs for the egg hunt, and their own dishes. Every child could bring a homemade Easter card to be given to the USO for a soldier overseas."

"The raised wooden platform Mimi uses for practicing her dance lessons would make an ideal stage for the storytellers," Aunt Lydia said. "We could put it in the center of the arena like a theatre in the round."

"Let's ask Aunt Hannah," I said, "if her music students would form a band and march in the parade."

Grandpa bent down and put the stack of records in the Victrola cabinet. "It's settled," he said abruptly. He strode over to his leather armchair, settled back comfortably in his chair, and grinned broadly. "We'll hold an Easter pageant at our farm, and I'll be the announcer."

"Thank you, Grandpa!" I shouted. Then I remembered reading that April was the rainiest month of the year. "Grandpa, what will we do if it rains?" I scowled.

"Mimi, don't be a worry-wart," Grandpa said. He laughed. "When we have a party at our farm, there's always sunshine. If it does rain I have lots of oilcloth tarps and umbrellas. When your Grandmother gets off the phone, I'll tell her all your suggestions."

"Grandpa, I was so excited about the prospect of winning a trophy, I didn't ask Charity if she wanted to be in the town's parade," I said remorsefully. "I'm going to apologize to her and find a way to include her in our pageant."

"That would be nice," Grandpa said. "However, be kind to yourself, honey. Charity doesn't hold grudges. Since you've been here, I've watched both of you blossom. Now, you'd better go to bed and get plenty of sleep. When your Grandmother comes home from that planning meeting tomorrow, she'll have a long list of chores for all of us." He chuckled. "Rest while you can."

"I'm so happy!" I said. "I can't wait to tell Charity about the pageant." I hugged Grandpa and Aunt Lydia goodnight.

Elated, I bounced up the stairs with faith and hope in my heart. Mom-Cat followed. Once in the Angel Room, I put Mom-Cat in her basket. Then I sat down at the rolltop desk and opened my story journal. *Oh, I forgot to ask Grandpa and Grandmother about the dressing table in the hayloft,* I thought. I picked up my pencil and rapidly jotted down ideas for the story contest. *Tomorrow, I'll solve that mystery.*

CHAPTER SEVEN

Secret Keepsakes

Immediately after breakfast on Good Friday, Grandpa drove Grandmother to the planning meeting at Aunt Hannah's house. Meanwhile, I had my riding lesson. By noon I had finished my lesson with Graceful Lady and was having fun riding Lilly in the arena when Grandpa's car pulled into the driveway. "Look!" I shouted to Aunt Lydia who was riding Freedom, Uncle Jim's Arabian horse. "Grandmother and Grandpa are home!"

"Would you please take Lilly and Freedom to their stalls?" Aunt Lydia asked. She quickly dismounted. "I'll find out the plans for Saturday, The Great Sabbath, and meet you at the barn."

Although bursting with curiosity, I nodded. "Whoa, Lilly." I eased her to a gentle halt, reluctantly climbed out of the saddle, and led Lilly and Freedom to their stalls. Mr. Jason was grooming Freedom, and I was in Lilly's stall cleaning her tack with a soft damp cloth when Aunt Lydia walked rapidly into the barn.

"Mimi, you've saved the day!" Aunt Lydia laughed.

"What do you mean?" I asked. I hung Lilly's bridle on the hook in her stall.

"The committee accepted all your suggestions," Aunt Lydia replied. "The Easter pageant starts at noon tomorrow at our farm. The first activity is the children's parade in the arena, followed by the story contest, potluck picnic, and egg hunt."

"I can't believe it." Dazed, I stood still and looked at Aunt Lydia.

"It's true," Aunt Lydia said in a cheery voice, showing me a neatly written program of the pageant's scheduled events and rules. "To make the contest more entertaining, the committee decided the storytellers are allowed to include their mounts in their presentation and have an assistant. The storytellers and their assistants are required to dress in a costume appropriate to their story. The time limit for each contestant is ten minutes or less. After the contest, the audience will vote for their favorite storyteller. The winner receives a gold trophy, and the runner-up gets a blue ribbon."

"This sounds exciting," I said.

"Grandmother and Aunt Hannah are busy as bees contacting families to invite them to the pageant and organizing a band," Aunt Lydia said. "Grandpa's at the house unloading chairs and tables for the pageant from the back of our truck." She looked at her watch pendant. "Mr. Timothy will be bringing Charity here soon for her lesson. I'm going to run to the house and call in a fabric order for the shop. I'll be back in a few minutes."

After I put Lilly's saddle in the tack room, I hurried to the back of the barn and climbed up the ladder to the hayloft. Now that I knew the plans for the pageant, I wanted to get the new flagpole and solve the mystery of the locked drawer.

I'll try to open the drawer with the biggest key, I thought. I took the key ring from the dressing table's secret compartment and inserted the key into the lock on the center drawer. It fit perfectly. I held my breath, turned the key, and tugged on the brass knob. "Ooh!" I cried. Inside the drawer was a wooden box about a foot long, six inches wide, and six inches deep. I wiped the thick layer of dust off the top of the box with my sleeve.

To my surprise, the lid's surface was decorated with a golden angel holding an open scroll with the words, "Love One Another" inscribed on it. I slipped the key ring over my wrist, took hold of the box, and gently lifted it from the drawer. A little rusty padlock secured the box.

"Mimi, are you in the loft, again?" Aunt Lydia shouted from below.

"Yes," I said. Clutching the box and the flagpole I slowly climbed down the ladder. "Yesterday, when I was looking for the pole, I found my great-grandmother's old dressing table. The center drawer was locked. Hidden in a secret compartment in another drawer were two rusty keys. I opened the drawer with one of the keys and found this box."

"Those steps are narrow. Be careful, Mimi," Aunt Lydia warned. "Let me help you." She stood at the bottom of the ladder and reached toward me with outstretched hands.

"The exact phrase Charity and I used for our banner's motto," I said, handing her the flagpole, "is engraved on the top of this box."

"How amazing," Aunt Lydia said. "Let's take the pole and box to the house and see if we can open it."

Then Aunt Lydia carried the flagpole and I carried the mysterious box into the kitchen.

"How long do you think this box has been hidden in the dressing table?" I asked, putting the box on the table.

Aunt Lydia closed the back door, stood the pole next to the kitchen corner cupboard, and turned toward me. "I don't know," she said with a perplexed expression. "We'll have to ask Grandpa and Grandmother. They drove to town to visit Mr. Moses and pick up some farm and household supplies." She sat down at the kitchen table and rubbed her fingers across the top of the box. "It might be an old music box designed to hold gloves, jewelry, or handkerchiefs."

I put the tiny key into the midget-sized rusty padlock and slowly turned it. The lock sprang open. Quickly, I removed it and lifted the lid. There were three loud clicking sounds, a whirring noise, and then silence.

A musty, stale odor rose from the box. Aunt Lydia and I coughed and sneezed. All I could see within the box was crumpled gray paper.

"It is an antique music box!" Aunt Lydia exclaimed. "But the music mechanism is broken."

"Look!" I said, carefully rummaging through the paper. "There's a leather drawstring pouch and a small white glass bowl shaped like an Easter basket. The pouch feels like it's stuffed with marbles." I handed the pouch and glass basket to Aunt Lydia.

"I've never seen such an unusual milk glass bowl," Aunt Lydia said. "It has a handle and the lid's designed like a nest with little chicks hatching from their eggs." She put the fragile glass basket and pouch on the table. "Is there anything else in the box?"

"There's a brown leather journal," I said, "a faded black and white photograph, and a wooden Easter egg. An empty cross and the date *Easter 1864* are carved on the egg." I placed the items on the table next to the pouch and glass basket.

"Mimi, the right bottom corner of this picture is signed *Catherine Marie Noble – 1864*," Aunt Lydia said, picking up the photograph. "This must be a picture of your great-grandmother when she was about your age." I leaned over Aunt Lydia's shoulder and stared at the photograph. A slender girl with a wistful smile, enormous eyes, smooth dark hair, wearing a Moravian outfit and cape was sitting sidesaddle astride a donkey. It seemed as though she was gazing back at us.

"In 1864, our country was torn apart by the Civil War," Aunt Lydia said in a grave tone. "Are there any entries in the journal?"

I opened the diary and slowly turned the yellowed pages. "There's only one handwritten note. It's on the second page. Some of the words are blurred."

I moved Grandpa's kitchen armchair closer to Aunt Lydia's chair, sat down, and read the entry to Aunt Lydia. "*Easter 1864 – Lititz, Pennsylvania. Father and I attended the Easter Sunrise Service. I wore my Moravian outfit for the children's program. I miss Nathaniel, my brother. We are proud he is a doctor and helping the wounded soldiers. Last week, Father gave one of our horses to the Pennsylvania cavalry. I am thankful for my little donkey and cart. This morning, Father surprised me with a small glass basket-shaped bowl, Mother's pearl necklace, bracelet, and ring. He said Mother wanted me to have these keepsakes. Father also gave me an Easter egg he had carved and a wooden music box. The words of my favorite Bible verse are etched on the top of the box. After church, Father and I put flowers on Mother's grave.*

We shall be happy when the War is over, and all will live in peace, love, and unity.

Catherine Marie Noble"

When I finished reading, I handed the journal to Aunt Lydia. "I wish I had known my great-grandmother. She was a girl when a war was going on and must have loved that Bible verse for the same reason I do."

Aunt Lydia pondered over the writing in the journal. "Your great-grandmother was an extraordinary girl. She made this entry during a time of personal loss and a turbulent year in our country's history." She sighed deeply. "After all these years we're still praying for peace."

"I have a picture, at home, of my great-grandmother. Now, I know what she looked like as a girl." I picked up the pouch and untied the drawstring. "I'm curious to see what's in this pouch."

"I'll hold the box," Aunt Lydia said, closing the journal and placing it on the table, "and you can pour whatever it is into it."

Clink! Clunk! Clink! Out from the pouch and into the box rolled the most beautiful pearls I'd ever seen, and a gleaming pearl bracelet. "Oh," I gasped. "These pearls must be from great-grandmother's necklace, and this is her bracelet."

"What a unique bracelet," Aunt Lydia said, holding the bracelet up to the light and examining it. "Look, a special clasp allows each of these two identical strands to be worn separately or joined to form one bracelet, and these cameos in the middle of each strand are profiles of old-fashioned Moravian ladies. The beauty of these delicately carved cameos and pearls is breathtaking."

"Let's put them back in the pouch so they won't get lost," I said. When the pearls and bracelet were back in the pouch, I took the little wooden egg from off the table and gently shook it. "There's something rattling inside." I swiftly twisted the egg open. Within the egg were a girl's gold ring and one small pearl. "Aunt Lydia, I found the ring, but the pearl is out of the setting."

"I think a jeweler could reset the pearl and restring the necklace," Aunt Lydia said, "and the music box could be repaired." She shook her head. "What priceless antique mementos you've discovered!"

For several minutes we sat quietly looking at the keepsakes on the table. The only sounds that could be heard were the crackling of the embers in Grandmother's coal stove and the ticking of the kitchen mantel clock.

All of a sudden I had an idea. "Aunt Lydia, can donkeys be in the parade and story contest?"

Aunt Lydia nodded. "Grandmother said horses, ponies, and donkeys were permitted in the pageant, however no other kinds of animals are allowed." She put the journal back in the box. "Why?"

"After seeing my great-grandmother's picture, I have a fantastic idea. I'm going to ask

Charity to wear her Moravian outfit and lead the parade riding Lilly sidesaddle," I said excitedly, "just like Jesus rode on the back of a donkey when He made His triumphant entry into Jerusalem." I put the ring and pearl in the wooden egg. "Charity can carry our banner, and I'll follow her riding Graceful Lady. For the story contest, Charity and I can wear our Moravian outfits and pretend to be early Moravian missionaries. I'll tell the Easter story, and Charity can be my helper and ride in Lilly's cart."

"But I thought one of your greatest desires," Aunt Lydia said with a puzzled expression, "was to lead the parade riding Graceful Lady."

"It was," I said, "before I realized Charity may have wanted to be in the parade, but thought participating was impossible. Maybe when the kids see Charity leading the parade, carrying our banner, and taking part in the contest they won't think of her as being disabled or different."

"I agree," Aunt Lydia said. "Most people tend to focus on what Charity can't do rather than on what she can do." She got up from the table and hugged me.

"Thanks, Aunt Lydia. Being in the pageant wouldn't be any fun without Charity and Lilly."

"However, the parade's tomorrow. The only time both of you will have to practice riding sidesaddle and using Lilly's cart is this afternoon," Aunt Lydia said as we put the items back in the music box. "While you're having lunch with Charity, I'll tack up Lilly and Graceful Lady, and ask Mr. Jason to get the cart out of the livery stable. Grandmother made some peanut butter and apple butter sandwiches and lemonade for you and Charity before she left and put them in the icebox."

Suddenly, a knocking sound at the kitchen door interrupted us.

"It's Charity," I said, glancing out the window. I hurried to place the box and key ring on top of the china cabinet and scooted to the door. "Come in, Charity," I said, opening the door. "You're just in time for lunch."

"Hello, Charity," Aunt Lydia said. She took a raisin oatmeal cookie from Grandmother's cookie jar. "I'll see you both at the arena."

While Charity and I sat at the kitchen table and ate lunch, I told her the town's parade was canceled, but Grandmother and Grandpa said we could have an Easter pageant at their farm on the Great Sabbath. I explained our pageant would include a children's parade, story contest, picnic, and an egg hunt.

"I'm sorry I didn't ask you if you wanted to be in the town's parade." I got up from my chair, walked over to Charity, and laid my hand on top of hers.

"It's all right," Charity said. "I didn't have a horse or pony to ride, and I couldn't have marched on foot."

"Would you like to be in the children's Easter parade tomorrow at Grandpa's farm?" I asked. "And help me with the story contest?"

"Oh, yes!" Charity's face flushed with happiness. Then she looked down at her legs and up at me. "But, how, Mimi?" Her eyes brimmed with tears. "I need my crutches to walk. The kids will snicker and laugh at me."

"You can wear your Moravian outfit and my long red cape, carry our banner, and lead the parade riding Lilly sidesaddle," I said. "Your skirt and the cape will cover your legs."

"But, you wanted to lead the parade," Charity said. She looked bewildered. "I've never ridden sidesaddle."

"Having you ride Lilly is a perfect way to start our Easter parade. It will remind people of how Jesus rode a donkey through the streets of Jerusalem. I'll wear my riding outfit and follow you riding Graceful Lady," I said reassuringly, "then close the parade carrying the banner. Aunt Lydia's going to teach us to ride sidesaddle this afternoon."

"What would I have to do in the contest?" Charity asked with a worried look. "My voice squeaks, my stomach gets in knots, and my hands shake when I have to talk in front of people."

"You won't have to say one word," I replied. "We'll both wear our Moravian outfits and pretend we're early Moravian missionaries who lived in Bethlehem long ago. I'll tell the

Easter story. All you have to do is ride in Lilly's cart, hold Patience, smile, and wave to the onlookers like a princess."

"I can do that," Charity said. She looked relieved and laughed. "Mimi, you've thought of everything."

"I hope so." I sighed. "Now, let's go out to the arena and rehearse our performance."

Leaning on her crutches, Charity got up from the kitchen chair. "I can't believe it," she said. "I'll actually be leading a parade."

Throughout the afternoon, Charity and I practiced riding sidesaddle and rehearsed for the contest under the watchful eyes of Aunt Lydia and Mr. Jason. At four o'clock, when Mr. Timothy came to take Charity home, Aunt Lydia and I told him all about the pageant.

"Goodbye, Charity. We're going to be the best team in the competition," I said, assisting her into the front seat of the car. "Don't forget the pageant starts at noon tomorrow. Remember to wear your Moravian outfit and bring some play clothes to wear for the egg hunt."

After Charity left, I went upstairs to the Angel Room. Filled with excitement and enthusiasm, I sat down at the desk, took out my journal, and wrote my story presentation. I made it exactly ten minutes long. I didn't want Charity and me to be disqualified for going over the allotted time. It was hard to concentrate. I kept glancing out the upstairs window waiting for Grandpa and Grandmother to come home. I wanted to show them the music box and tell them about my plans for the pageant. When they finally came home, I ran downstairs to meet them at the kitchen door. Grandpa asked me to help unload the car and put the groceries in the kitchen pantry while Grandmother put the teakettle on the stove to boil and brewed a fresh pot of coffee.

"Mimi, on our way home from town," Grandpa said, sitting down at the kitchen table with a cup of coffee and a doughnut, "Grandmother and I stopped at the hospital to see Mr. Moses. He told us he and his wife were selling their farm for health reasons and moving to Nazareth to live with their daughter. Of course, I offered to buy Lilly, her tack, and cart." Grandpa chuckled. "Mr. Moses accepted my offer, and Lilly is now part of our family."

"Oh, Grandpa! That's wonderful! Will you put her name on the plaque above her stall?"

"Lilly can stay in that stall," Grandpa said, "and I'll paint her name on the plaque and stall door."

Then I told Grandmother and Grandpa about my plans for the parade, how I found the music box, and the keepsakes hidden inside it.

"That antique dressing table and matching chair have been stored in the loft for years," Grandmother said, inspecting the pearl jewelry. "We had no idea a treasure was hidden in one of the drawers." She smiled.

Grandpa picked up my great-grandmother's photograph, studied it, and looked intently at me. He grinned. "Mimi, I think you look like your great-grandmother."

"Grandmother and Grandpa, I know the pearl bracelet is old and valuable," I said. "But could I please keep one strand, and give the other to Charity? It would make a perfect friendship bracelet."

"The bracelet is a priceless and unique family heirloom," Grandmother said. She looked thoughtful. "However, it would be a lovely gift for Charity and appropriate, since the cameos are of a Moravian lady."

"It's not doing any good stored in a box gathering dust," Grandpa said. "Knowing Charity, she'll take good care of her half of the bracelet and cherish it forever."

"Thank you, Grandmother and Grandpa," I said gratefully.

"Mimi, while you and Grandmother are putting the items in a safe place and preparing supper," Grandpa said, "I'll drive downtown to the jewelry store, have the jeweler check the bracelet, and see if he can repair the necklace and ring." Grandpa put on his jacket and hat, and stuck the leather pouch into his pocket.

Later, when Grandmother and I were setting the kitchen table, Grandpa opened the back door and burst into the kitchen. "Mimi, I have good news," Grandpa said. He shut the door, hung up his coat and hat, and turned toward me. "The jeweler was able to clean and repair the bracelet. I had him put each strand in a separate black velvet jewelry box." He handed me two little boxes.

"Thank you," I said. "I can't wait to give Charity her half of the bracelet." I hugged Grandpa and Grandmother. "I'm putting these boxes upstairs on the bureau in the Angel Room."

"On your way to your room," Grandmother said, "please tell Aunt Lydia supper will be ready in ten minutes. She's in the sitting room writing a letter to your Uncle Jim. You might want to bring your hat, gloves, and Bible downstairs. By the time we're through eating it will be time for church."

That evening after the church service, Grandmother, Aunt Lydia, and I dyed and decorated Easter eggs.

Later, on my way upstairs to bed, I stopped in the sitting room to say goodnight to Grandpa and Grandmother. "Grandpa, may I use one of your lanterns tomorrow for the story contest?"

"Certainly, honey. I always keep them on the kitchen shelf by the door."

"Thank you, Grandpa." I climbed halfway up the stairs, stopped, leaned over the cherry wood banister, and blew Grandmother and Grandpa a kiss. "You're the best grandparents in the whole world."

When I entered the Angel Room I placed my scarlet riding jacket, jodhpurs, white blouse, and Moravian outfit neatly on the Windsor chair by the desk. Then I stood Aunt Lydia's high leather riding boots by the bedroom door. I didn't want to waste time looking for anything tomorrow morning. Exhausted, I put on my nightclothes, switched off the light, and crept into bed. But before going to sleep, I rolled up in the soft down coverlet like a cozy cocoon and told Patience, my teddy bear, and Mom-Cat the Easter story as golden moonbeams streamed through the window and danced on my bed.

CHAPTER EIGHT

Everybody Loves a Parade

On The Great Sabbath, I awoke before the crack of dawn. Eager for the day to begin, I leaped out of bed, braided my hair, and dressed in my riding outfit. I took a pearl strand from one of the jewelry boxes, slipped it over my wrist, and put the other box in my pocket. Mom-Cat, laying in her basket, yawned, stretched, and went back to sleep. I hugged my teddy bear and Patience and slipped them back under the covers. Buttoning my jacket I tiptoed to the top of the steps. Then I rushed downstairs and bolted out the kitchen door to the backyard to check the weather. Grandpa and Mr. Jason were walking toward the house. "Good morning," I called to them. I ran straight across the lawn into Grandpa's wide-open arms. "Tomorrow is the last day of my Easter vacation. May I please ring the bell?"

Grandpa nodded. "Just give the handle on the bell's rope two hard yanks." He hugged me tightly. "Mimi, we're going to miss your sparkling eyes and sunny smile."

"Thanks, Grandpa." I scooted from his arms and pulled the rope.

DING-DONG! DING-DONG! The bell pealed. "Rise and shine!" I cried while Grandpa and Mr. Jason stood by and watched. "You were right about the weather, Grandpa." I wound the bell's rope and hung it on the post. "It's not raining, and the weather vane on top of the barn's roof isn't moving."

"It's going to be a splendid day for a parade," Grandpa said. Mr. Jason nodded as we walked to the farmhouse.

Mom, Dad, and Matt arrived in time for breakfast. During our tasty meal of ham and eggs, hash brown potatoes, buttermilk biscuits, and coffee cake, Grandpa, Grandmother, and I told them about our upcoming Easter pageant.

When we were finished eating, Mrs. Jason, Grandmother, and Mom started making hot potato salad, baked ribs and sauerkraut, and shoo-fly pie for the day's festivities. Dad and Matt went out to the backyard to set up tables for the picnic and arrange chairs and benches around the outside of the arena for the spectators. In the meantime, Grandpa and Mr. Jason hurried to raise the American flag in the backyard, get Lilly's cart out from the livery stable, move the wooden riser platform to the center of the arena, and attach our banner to the new pole.

Amid the flurry of preparation, Aunt Lydia and I scampered to the barn to groom and tack up Lilly and Graceful Lady.

Aunt Lydia curried Graceful Lady, and I brushed Lilly's coat until it glistened like velvet. "Lilly, Mr. and Mrs. Moses are moving. Our family loves you, so from now on Grandpa's farm is your new home!" I said, patting her neck. "Today, you and Charity are going to be the stars of the pageant." Lilly rolled her big, dark brown eyes skyward, held her ears up straight as peppermint sticks, and grinned, showing all her lily-white teeth.

Later, when Grandpa, Mr. Jason, Aunt Lydia, and I emerged from the barn leading Graceful Lady and Lilly, the yard and meadow swarmed with laughing, excited children. Matt and Mark were sitting on the back porch steps taking turns cranking the handle of the wooden ice cream bucket. I waved to them as we walked Lilly and Graceful Lady to the arena's wide entrance gate.

"Hello," Charity called to us from the bench by the gate. "My Dad's helping your Uncle Luke and Aunt Hannah get the band members ready. I didn't sleep a wink last night. I kept thinking about the pageant."

"I'm glad you came early," I said. "The parade is starting in a few minutes. The kids are lining up in the meadow. From there, they'll march to this gate, follow us as we circle the inside of the arena, and exit after us through this same gate."

"Charity, you look lovely in your Moravian dress," Aunt Lydia said. She secured Graceful Lady and Lilly to the hitching post. Then she tucked Charity's tousled golden curls under her white linen cap, and tied the bright red ribbons in a perky bow under her chin. "Now, let's get you mounted on Lilly."

I held onto Lilly's bridle while Grandpa picked Charity up from the bench and set her on Lilly's sidesaddle. Aunt Lydia came forward and draped my long red cape around Charity's shoulders.

"Cassandra's wearing a cowgirl outfit and riding her Shetland pony in the parade," Charity said with an anxious expression. "I saw her in the meadow with her pony." She looked down at her legs. "Can you see my braces?"

"Your dress and cape completely cover your legs," Aunt Lydia said reassuringly as she adjusted the stirrup.

I laughed. "Cassandra's in for a big surprise when she sees you leading the parade."

"Ladies, if you'll excuse me I need to talk to the pageant chairman," Grandpa said, surveying the crowd, "and see if there are enough chairs around the arena for the spectators. It looks like half the town is here."

After Grandpa left, I took the black jewelry box from my pocket. "Charity, I have a gift for you." I handed her the little velvet box.

Charity slowly opened the box. "Oh!" she exclaimed. "It's a beautiful pearl bracelet."

"It's one strand of a pearl bracelet and exactly like the strand I'm wearing. The strands can be worn separately or joined to form one bracelet. The cameo is of a Moravian lady. This bracelet is over a hundred years old and belonged to my great-grandmother," I explained. "Now it's our special friendship bracelet."

"Thank you," Charity whispered. She lifted the pearl strand from the velvet cushion, wrapped it around her wrist, and closed the clasp. Then she raised her arm to admire the bracelet. The iridescent pearls caught the sun's rays and shimmered and sparkled in the sunlight. "No one has ever given me anything this pretty." She wiped tears from her eyes. "This bracelet will always remind me we are true friends."

"And sisters, forever," I added.

Just then the pageant chairman, standing on the platform in the center of the arena with Grandpa, blew three loud shrill blasts on his trumpet. It was the signal for the pageant to begin. After Grandpa welcomed our friends, neighbors, and guests to the farm and read from the Bible, everyone stood up, faced the American flag on the platform, and put their right hand over their heart. The boys and men took off their hats, and we all said The Pledge of Allegiance and sang "The Star-Spangled Banner." When everybody was seated, Grandpa grinned widely and gestured toward the entrance gate.

"Charity Timothy mounted on Lilly," he announced, "will lead the parade carrying a banner proclaiming the pageant's theme, 'Love One Another.' Mimi Noble will close the parade carrying the same banner."

All heads turned toward the entrance gate.

"Mimi, everyone's staring at us!" Charity gasped. Her face turned white. She shuddered, dropped the reins, and slouched forward in the saddle.

"Please don't get stage fright and faint," I said, handing her our banner, "or I'll never forgive myself." I sighed. "Charity, take a deep breath, act like a princess, and hold onto the banner's pole and Lilly's reins."

"I won't faint." Then she giggled. In an instant Charity regained her composure. Sitting erect in the saddle and whispering encouragingly to Lilly, she steered her forward through the entrance gate and into the arena. A sudden gust of wind caught our brilliant banner. It opened in the breeze and displayed our motto for everyone to see.

Aunt Lydia helped me mount Graceful Lady, and I followed Charity into the arena. I glanced over my shoulder at the procession following me and at the crowd surrounding the arena. All the kids were gaping at Charity with amazed expressions and disbelief in their eyes, while the grown-ups smiled, nodded approvingly, and applauded. "Today," I said to Graceful Lady, "Lilly and Charity are going to have center stage." As if understanding me, Graceful Lady slowed her gait, whinnied gleefully, and tossed her mane back and forth. "Good girl," I said, stroking her neck.

Matt and Mark marched in back of me. They both carried large American flags.

Next came the children's band playing patriotic music led by a boy and a girl twirling silver batons. Behind the band, kids of all ages marched on foot or rode gaily decorated bikes, scooters, or wagons. After the wagons, there were clowns and jugglers tossing balls and hoops high in the air. Then came two girls wearing red, white, and blue costumes riding prancing ponies. Cassandra followed them, dressed in a cowgirl outfit, riding her Shetland pony. Three boys on horseback brought up the rear. One, wearing a pirate's costume, had a black patch over his eye. The other two, dressed like cowboys, twirled lassoes.

When Charity and I had circled the inside of the arena and were back at the gate, Mr. Timothy lifted Charity from Lilly's saddle and set her back on the bench. "For the first time in my life," Charity called to me, "I felt people saw me, and not my braces or crutches." Her eyes sparkled as bright as Grandmother's Moravian crystal star ornaments.

"Hurray!" I shouted. So far everything was running smoothly.

I quickly dismounted Graceful Lady, tied her to the post, took the banner from Charity, and climbed onto Lilly's sidesaddle. When all the parade participants had finished marching around the arena, Lilly and I closed the parade amid cheers to a standing ovation. Back at the gate, I jumped off Lilly, handed the reins and banner to Aunt Lydia, and ran to the house to change into my Moravian outfit for the contest.

When I returned with Patience, my Bible, some palm branches, and Grandpa's lantern, Lilly was hitched to the cart. Charity, radiant and happy, was sitting on the front seat, and our banner was attached to the side of the cart.

"Mimi, while you were at the house," Aunt Lydia said, "the judges announced only three other children are entering the story contest. Cassandra is first; next are two boys. You and Charity are last."

Charity sat patiently in the cart while the contestants performed with their horses and ponies. I was on pins and needles. I tried to stand still, listen to their presentations, and not fidget.

Finally it was our turn. "Charity, our performance will be exactly like we rehearsed it," I said. I handed her Patience, the Bible, and the palm branches. "All you have to do is hold the Bible and wave the branches to the crowd. I'll carry the lantern. Patience can keep you company."

"I'm ready, Mimi," Charity said, sitting Patience on her lap.

"Here we go!" I took hold of Lilly's lead rope and we entered the arena.

"Girls," Aunt Lydia called after us, "you both look like the Moravian ladies carved on your cameos. Mr. Timothy and I will stand by the gate and watch your presentation. We'll be cheering for you."

When our cart was in the center of the arena, I brought Lilly to a halt and Grandpa introduced us to the audience. Holding Lilly's rope, I stepped onto the platform, smiled, and curtsied. "Ladies and gentlemen, girls and boys," I said loudly so everyone could hear me, "Charity and I are dressed like the brave early Moravian missionaries, who left their homes in Bethlehem, and traveled all over the Pennsylvania territory to take the Gospel to the Indians and pioneers. So please use your imagination, pretend you're living a long time ago, in the 1700's, and gather round while I tell the Easter story."

At the conclusion of my story, I pointed at Lilly. "Our donkey's name is Lilly. She doesn't know any stunts or tricks," I explained, "but she's gentle, humble, sure-footed on the road, and never balks or grumbles. She happily hauls or carries heavy loads as we go throughout the land sharing the Good News with everyone we meet. So let us all take a stand to follow our Lord's command to love one another. Then wars will cease, and everyone will live in unity and peace." I curtsied and led Lilly with Charity in the cart to the gate. Charity didn't stop waving and smiling at the applauding audience until Mr. Timothy lifted her from the cart, and she was leaning on her crutches.

"Mimi and Charity, you were spectacular! I'm proud of you," Aunt Lydia said, embracing us. "Mr. Timothy and I will unhitch Lilly from the cart, while you're changing your clothes." Immediately, Charity and I went to the house. I put on my riding outfit and Charity changed into her play clothes.

Later, after everyone feasted on the delicious potluck meal and voted for their favorite storyteller, the ballots were tallied. The pageant chairman, standing in the middle of the arena by Grandpa, blew his trumpet and handed Grandpa a sealed envelope containing the winning names. Grandpa ripped open the envelope, cleared his throat, and announced the second place winner. Everyone clapped when Grandpa presented a blue and gold ribbon to the boy dressed like a pirate. "Folks, the first place winner is," Grandpa paused, "Mimi Noble! Would you please come forward, Mimi, and claim the gold trophy." He grinned widely.

"Ooh!" I exclaimed. Thrilled, I jumped from my chair. I turned and hugged Mom and Dad, who were seated next to Charity and me, and hustled through the maze of people, chairs, and tables to the platform. "Thank you," I said to the crowd. "I'd like to have Charity accept this trophy with me." I flashed a wide smile at her. "Without Charity's help, I couldn't have won this trophy."

Suddenly, a hush came over the audience. Charity blushed and pushed herself up from her chair. With happy, shining eyes she smiled at the audience. Then, with her head held high and using her crutches, she shuffled to the arena's gate. I ran to meet her, flung my arms around her in a joyous hug, and guided her to the platform. Proud and triumphant, we raised the brilliant gold trophy high over our heads. Lilly, tethered to an apple tree in the orchard, brayed loudly, "hee-haw, hee-haw." Everyone laughed, rose from their seats, and broke into a thunderous burst of applause. Then all the kids gathered around Charity and me and congratulated us on winning the trophy. Cassandra, red-faced and misty-eyed, made her way slowly through the crowd, stepped up on the platform, and faced Charity. "I'm sorry," she whispered, looking into Charity's eyes, "for being thoughtless and mean. Can you forgive me?" She put her hands over Charity's. "Would you like to join our riding club?"

Charity nodded. "Yes, I forgive you." She glowed with happiness. "And I'd love to be a member of your club."

"Girls and boys," Grandpa announced, taking his gold pocket watch out from his pocket, "it's time for the egg hunt. Let's all go to the orchard and see who can find the most eggs in fifteen minutes. Then it will be time to collect the handmade Easter cards for the soldiers, clean up, and go to the evening service."

That evening at church, Mom and Dad, Matt, Mark, Charity, and I shared the front pew with Mr. and Mrs. Jason. During the Lovefeast Service, Grandpa, Uncle Luke, and Mr. Timothy helped distribute the mugs of hot coffee and chocolate to the congregation. Grandmother and Aunt Lydia, dressed in white and wearing small white caps, passed the baskets of sweet buns.

"Mimi, I'll never forget today and these past two weeks," Charity said after the service, as we stood in the church foyer. "You made it the happiest time of my life. When the kids were rude or ignored me, you understood how I felt and were kind."

"I'll always remember this Easter vacation, too. You taught me how to turn our motto into action. I learned love starts with being a friend," I said, taking our coats from the foyer closet, "and our Easter pageant turned out better than I could have ever imagined. Tomorrow, after the Sunrise Service and children's program, I have to go home."

"I'll miss you," Charity said softly.

"I'll be back in July. Our family always celebrates the Fourth of July at Grandpa's farm. While I'm gone, please help Grandpa take good care of Lilly and continue your riding lessons."

"I promise," Charity said, "and I'll wear my friendship bracelet on special occasions as it is so precious."

"I'll wear mine, too." I helped Charity into her coat. "Because we're true, loyal friends and sisters, forever!"

CHAPTER NINE

A Sunrise Surprise

Thump! Thump! Thump! Footsteps tramping down the stairs roused me from a sound sleep. Groggy and blurry-eyed I slid out of bed, turned on the light, and looked at the clock. *It's two o'clock on Easter morning. Grandpa is on his way with his trombone to God's Acre, the Moravian graveyard by the church,* I thought, taking my Moravian outfit out of the closet. *From God's Acre, Grandpa and the other musicians in the Brass Choir will walk through town playing Easter chorales to wake the members of our church for the Sunrise Service. If I hurry, I'll have time to say goodbye to Lilly and start packing before we leave for church.* I quickly put on my Moravian outfit, combed my hair, and slipped on my gold cross necklace and pearl friendship bracelet.

"Happy Easter, Patience, teddy bear, and Mom-Cat," I said cheerfully. "Let's all go to the barn and see Lilly." But, there was no answering meow from Mom-Cat.

I glanced down at her basket on the floor between the dresser and the desk. It was empty.

"Oh, no!" I cried. "Mom-Cat, where are you?" Frantically, I searched every nook and cranny of the room. Mom-Cat was nowhere to be found. I scooped up Patience and my teddy bear from off my bed. Clutching them and my Bible, I raced down stairs to the kitchen. The aroma of fresh perked coffee mixed with spicy smells of cinnamon, ginger, and nutmeg filled the kitchen. Aunt Lydia, in a long blue chenille robe, was taking Moravian hot cross buns and sugar cake from the oven.

"Aunt Lydia, I can't find Mom-Cat," I wailed. "She's not in my room. Have you seen her?"

"Not since last night," Aunt Lydia said, wrinkling her brow. She took the coffee pot off the stove and set it on a trivet on the kitchen table. "Mom-Cat might be in the barn with Lilly and Cuddly-Bell."

I snatched my red cape from the coat rack by the door and slipped it over my outfit. "I'm going to the barn to try to find her."

"I'll go with you," Aunt Lydia said. "It's chilly and pitch black outside. We'll need Grandpa's large lantern and the smaller one." She took the kerosene lanterns off the shelf and lit them. Carrying the small lantern, Patience, and my teddy bear, I darted out the back door. Aunt Lydia tossed Grandmother's wool shawl around her shoulders, grabbed the other lantern, and followed me out into the cold darkness.

Aunt Lydia and I were shivering, and my teeth were chattering when we reached the barn. I unlatched the door, grasped the handle, and yanked it open far enough for us to squeeze through. Once we were inside, I swiftly pulled the door shut. The yellow light flickering from the lanterns cast eerie black shadows on the stonewalls. The cows and horses stared at us in the feeble light with sleepy, bewildered eyes. "Mom-Cat, are you in here?" I called. Aunt Lydia and I clung to each other, stood still, and listened.

All of a sudden, I heard a soft meow coming from Lilly's stall. I ran from Aunt Lydia's side and opened the stall door. I couldn't believe my eyes. On the floor, curled up in Grandmother's clothesbasket, lay Mom-Cat and five tiny newborn kittens. Dozing by the door were Pretzel, Cuddly-Bell, and Crystal while Lilly, awake and alert, stood like a silent sentinel guarding Mom-Cat and her precious kittens. "Aunt Lydia, come quick!" I shouted. "Come and see Mom-Cat's kittens."

"Now we know why Mom Cat wouldn't come when you called her," Aunt Lydia said, walking into Lilly's stall.

I put Patience, teddy bear, and my Bible on a nearby bale of hay and hung the lantern on the wall hook. "Congratulations, Mom-Cat!" I stooped to pet her. "Your kittens are beautiful." Mom-Cat looked up at me and purred. "I'm proud of you for being a good mother and not leaving your kittens. I can't wait to show them to Charity and Mr. Sampson."

"I'd like to see the expression on Mr. Sampson's face when he delivers your mail, and you present him with a basket filled with five darling little kittens." Aunt Lydia laughed heartily. "Since Mom-Cat is safe and sound I'm going back to the house, wake everyone, and get ready for the Sunrise Service. I'll take a lantern and leave the other one for you."

After Aunt Lydia left, I gave Mom-Cat a light kiss on the top of her head and stood up. I looked down at my apron. *Oh!* I thought. *My apron and cape are covered with pieces of hay. I better brush them before I go into Grandmother's clean kitchen.* I took the lantern off the hook and set it on the stall's shelf. There, next to the brushes were my great-grandmother's music box, photograph, and a large Easter basket decorated with purple ribbons and stuffed with golden, sweet smelling straw. In the middle of the basket, encircled by colorful Easter eggs, stood a small, dark brown corduroy donkey wearing a blue and yellow saddle blanket, tan saddle, and halter. Also within the basket were two hand carved wooden eggs, my great-grandmother's basket-shaped bowl, leather journal, and a card addressed to me. Curious, I quickly took the card from the basket, huddled close to the lantern, and read the handwritten note.

To our dear granddaughter, Mimi,

This sunrise surprise is for you! Since Easter is a time of hope, faith, newness, and memories, Grandpa and I want you to have and enjoy these heirloom keepsakes and new handmade gifts.

Happy Easter! We love you!

Grandmother and Grandpa Noble

P.S. We had the music box repaired for you.

Bursting with curiosity to hear the melody the music box played, I laid the note on the shelf and lifted the lid. Immediately, the strains of the children's hymn, "Jesus Loves Me," filled the stall. As the music continued playing, I took the toy donkey out from the basket. "You look exactly like Lilly, with your black wool mane and tail, big ears, and black button eyes." I hugged the soft, little donkey and stood her next to Patience and my teddy bear. "You're the perfect size for Patience to ride."

Then, I carefully removed the top from the milk glass bowl. "Ooh!" I exclaimed. "Grandpa and Grandmother had the pearl necklace restrung." Delighted, I took the lovely necklace from the bowl and wrapped it around my neck. Next, I picked up the wooden eggs and quickly opened the one carved with a cross and the date, *Easter 1864*. Within the egg was the gold ring with the single lustrous pearl mounted in its setting. I slipped the

ring on the third finger of my right hand. It was a perfect fit. Inscribed on the other hand carved egg, were the words: *Mimi's Sunrise Surprise, Easter – 1944.* Laughing, I twisted it open and inside was the tiniest white-leather bound Bible I had ever seen. *Now, I'll have a Bible to carry with me every where I go,* I thought, tucking it in my pocket. Thrilled and thankful for my gifts, I placed the wooden eggs in my Easter basket and closed the lid of the music box.

Suddenly, I spun around on my heel. "Listen," I shouted. I took the lantern off the shelf and raced toward the front of the barn. I flung both doors wide open and looked up at the dark sky. A silver moon and shimmering stars peeked through billowing clouds promising a beautiful sunrise. "Listen, Mom-Cat, Pretzel, Crystal, Lilly, Cuddly-Bell, teddy bear, little donkey, and Patience. If you're still, you can hear the Brass Choir playing Easter chorales as they march through town. The music is a message to everyone to rejoice for the Lord is risen and to LOVE ONE ANOTHER!"

MIMI'S SUNRISE SURPRISE

To order books or schedule an appearance contact:

Joan M. Thomas, Author/Illustrator

P.O. Box 13063

Des Moines, WA 98198

Phone: (253) 315-9280

www.mimisgift.com